Something off-beat was going on.

Out of sheer boredom, thousands of unemployed Lagrangists were joining up so that they could wear the striking new uniforms that had been devised by the Sons of Liberty and participate in the parades, demonstrations and rallies. Sheer boredom can be a powerful force. How long would it be before the foe would decide they could swing the vote of a majority of the Lagrangists and call for a referendum?

Rex was on his return to the apartment and passing a heavily shaded park when the attack was made.

He could hear the bike approaching from behind him but it didn't occur to Rex to turn and look. Bicyclists weren't exactly a rarity on the streets of New Frisco, and violence was almost unheard of.

Suddenly, a burning, agonizing, tearing blow struck his right side and down he went toward the pavement of the sidewalk. Even as he fell, he recognized what had happened. He'd been hit, albeit glancingly, by a laser beam. A laser weapon in Lagrangia! It had already begun, and soon there would be

CHAOS IN
LAGRANGIA

BY MACK REYNOLDS

TOR

A TOM DOHERTY ASSOCIATES BOOK

CHAOS IN LAGRANGIA

This is a work of fiction. All the characters and events portrayed in this book are fictional, and any resemblance to real people or incidents is purely coincidental.

A TOR Book

Published by Tom Doherty Associates, Inc., 8-10 West 36th Street, New York, New York 10018

First TOR printing: March 1984

ISBN: 812-55-128-1
Can. Ed.: 812-55-129-X

Cover art by: Alan Gutierrez

Printed in the United States of America

Man will not always stay on Earth; the pursuit of light and space will lead him to penetrate the bounds of the atmosphere, timidly at first, but in the end to conquer the whole of solar space.
—Konstantin Tsiolkowsky, 1857–1935
    The Father of Space Colonization
    Taken from the obelisk marking
    his grave in Kuluga

CHAOS IN LAGRANGIA

Chapter One

King Ford wheeled his bike out through the suburbs of New Frisco and into the foothills beyond. It was a glorious day but he didn't notice that. The fact was, King Ford had never in his life of approximately a quarter of a century ever witnessed a less-than-glorious day. Oh, the Island of his birth had a somewhat warmer climate than did Grissom, which inclined more to the European-New England temperatures, but all days were perfect in both Islands. He understood that Komarov, the sister cylinder of Grissom, connected by cables on which they rotated, together making up Island Three of Lagrangia, actually had a tropical climate and one of its more attractive towns was pseudo-Polynesian, complete to grass huts and outrigger canoes pulled up on the beach of a quite sizeable lake. He had heard that most of the Lagrangists living there made a policy of wearing sarongs and grass skirts and going barefooted during off-work hours. If he possibly could, he'd have to take a trip over to Komarov and spend a few days there. There was nothing like a tropical village in the Asteroid Federation.

But Grissom was itself pleasurable enough for him and beyond his experience. His own home, Promised Land Three, was the largest Island in the asteroid belt but only about half the size of Grissom. Looking back over his shoulder, he could see down one of the two mile-wide 'valleys' far into the distance. The cylinder was some twenty miles in length and clouds prevented him from making out the other end but he had never seen so far before inside an Island. Grissom's cylinder circumference was divided into six regions, three valleys alternating with three arrays of tinted windows. It was the same arrangement as the Promised Land Islands though on a larger scale. For instance, from where he rode now, he could look up and see the other two valleys; but at a distance of four miles, the diameter of Grissom, he could make out practically nothing smaller than the larger towns.

He was heading in the direction of the tallest of the mountains which rose at the end-cap of the cylinder. It looked to be about ten thousand feet in altitude—very impressive. Toward the top, he assumed, you'd be near enough the axis that it would be almost zero-gravity.

King Ford had emerged from the suburbs into countryside which soon evolved into one of the parks usually dubbed wilderness in the space colonies. It was as well-done as he'd ever seen, even in the Tri-Di films brought up from Earthside of virgin forests. To add authenticity, a rabbit broke from a bush and scampered madly from the danger he thought threatened him. King Ford wondered how wide a variety of wildlife had been seeded here; probably more than at home.

The road become little more than a path and continued to wind along a stream coming down from the mountains. The way steepened but he found no difficulty in pedalling. Why should he? The more he ascended, the less the gravity. He probably could have left the bicycle at this point to run, or rather bound, the rest of the way up the peak.

But then King spotted the one he sought.

The other was an elderly man in his mid-sixties and was seated on a small overturned rowboat by the side of the stream, fishing pole in hand, eyes intent on the cork at the end of his line. His hair was gray but full and, given his years, his body seemed trim and in good shape. He didn't exactly make a handsome old man but he had a certain wistful, vulnerable quality about eyes and mouth that had its attractions.

King Ford dismounted and pushed his bike a little closer and said, "Mr. Bader?"

The other looked up. "Bader?" he said. "It's been a while since I've heard that, son. My name's currently Rex M-E-O-60-HLl." He frowned and said, "You must not be a Lagrangist, but haven't I seen you somewhere before?"

They spoke in Interlingua, the language of space.

The younger man grinned and propped his bike against a tree, which stood against the stream.

"You're thinking of my father," he said. "I'm King Ford."

"You mean you're Whip Ford's boy? Why, Holy Zen, sit down, son. How is Whip? I haven't heard from him in years but for a long time we kept in touch."

"Dad was fine when I saw him last, about a year ago." The younger man seated himself on a rock.

"He still out at the Promised Land?"

"Yes, of course. He'll never leave. It's his dream realized."

"It ought to be. He damned near pushed the building of it through all by himself. Your father was a good man, son. What'd you say your name was?"

"King Ford," the other said, and frowned. "What was that you called yourself instead of Bader? I suppose that I've got a lot to learn about places other than the asteroid belt. I'm a tourist, you know."

"It's the system of naming that they've worked out here," the old man told him. "The old way was inefficient. The name told you practically nothing, not even, in many cases, the sex of the bearer. Some first names were used for either sex, such as Billy, Frances and Dallas, and there were as many female Pats around as males. Then, especially in Catholic countries, you'd have Marie, Claude, Alexandre, Jaime, and Jane, which could be either. And the last name was meaningless even so far as denoting relationship. There could be thousands of Smiths, largely unrelated to each other, in the phone book of a major city."

"Well, how does the new system work?"

"My name's Rex, which is what everybody calls me. Then my last name, my official name, in all the records, is M-E-O-60-HLl. Than means M, I'm a male. E, I was born on Earth; O is my blood type, 1960 is the year of my birth. Then you have my identification number, usually a couple of letters and four numbers in length, but I'm an exception. My number is HL1. That means Honorary Lagrangist and since there's only one, I'm that number."

"Honorary Lagrangist?"

"That's right." The older man made a quick flick of his wrist, a split second after his cork had disappeared, and jerked his line out of the water. The hook was empty of either fish or bait. "Damn," he muttered. "Either these specks are getting smarter, or I'm slowing up."

He laid the fishing tackle on the bank's edge and turned back to the youth. "They made me an Honorary Lagrangist, in spite of the fact I didn't have the qualifications, by special action of the Grand Council, after your father and I participated in a little difficulty here back in the old days."

"He told me about it."

Rex cocked his head a little. "You know, you do look like your father. Maybe not quite so dark. I used to be quite a buff for the old revival movies and I used to make kind of a hobby identifying people by comparison to some old time movie actors. I used to think Whip looked like Harry Belafonte. He was a handsome man, back when I knew him. Has he still got that chip on his shoulder against whities?"

King laughed. "No, I suppose he got over that by the time the Promised Land was completed and colonized by blacks only, supposedly to get away from racial Earthside discrimination. For one thing, so many of the technicians from Lagrangia who came out to help in building our space colony were white and did such a damn good job that it was hard not to take to them."

"Wizard," Rex said gruffly. "There's no room in space for that sort of Earthside racism crud."

The young man shrugged. "Then after more Islands were developed in the asteroid belt, we formed a loose confederation, for mutual help. Each Island sends one delegate. Dad has been our representative since the Federation was first started and he works with whites all of the time. They've done him the honor of making him chairman."

The old man said, "I don't keep up with developments as much as I should, I suppose. The asteroid belt's so far away. How many Islands are out there now?"

"Nine finished, one abuilding. A couple being planned."

"Holy Zen. In just the twenty-five years or so since your father started the Promised Land? All settled by blacks? But no, you said there were whites in your Federation."

"That's right. We were just the first. We built a small Island suitable for about 10,000 colonists, very similar to the Lagrange Five Island One. Then, as more colonists came up from Earth, and as children began to be born, we built two more Islands about the size of your Island Twos." King looked up and around, at Grissom in general. "Now we're planning to build one as large as this. But we're not alone. Before we'd even finished our first Island, some Chinese came up and started on Han. They were largely from places like Hong Kong, Singapore, San Francisco. They didn't like Communist China and didn't like the way their culture was disappearing. So they decided to take the old ways up into space. Working like madmen—or Chinese—they had Han finished in chopchop time and started in on Ming which is Island Two size."

"Chinese, eh?" Rex said. "Who else?"

"Then there's Penn, kind of settled by the equivalent of the Pennsylvania Amish. Back to the simple life. It's rather amusing. To keep a space colony operating, of course, you've got to use the very latest in technology. So they work all day as scientists and engineers and so forth, and then go home to the most fantastic old-fashioned ways; church suppers, knitting bees, plowing with horses, nineteenth century clothing, and all the rest. However, they seem to be happy enough, like an oversized commune, I suppose. They're something like Victoria, another Island in the asteroids."

"Victoria?"

"That's right. Back to the old values of the Victorian age. Back to classical capitalism, so far as political economy is concerned. Then there's Pericles, the most far-out of all. Devoted to the arts. How they ever keep it going, I'll never know. More far-outs per square foot than Athens ever dreamed of during the Golden Age. Then there's Marx, which isn't finished yet. They're still working on it and of course all the rest of us cooperate. Bunch of Earthside radicals who are bound and determined to establish pure scientific socialism."

"Let's see," Rex said. "That leaves one unaccounted for."

"Umm," the other told him unhappily. "Elysium. She's currently not a member of the Asteroid Federation."

"Why not?"

"Well . . ." King Ford still looked unhappy, as though he wasn't quite sure how to put it. "Elysium was originally built by anarchists. Zen only knows where they raised the money."

Rex scratched a thumb over the stubble on his chin. He said, "My father used to teach socioeconomics and some of it rubbed off on me. You'd be surprised how many of the early anarchists weren't exactly poor. Tolstoy, for instance, was a count and Prince Peter Kropotkin was, of course, a prince. I think even Percy Shelley had some kind of title but whether or not, he wasn't exactly penniless."

King said, "At any rate, they were idealistic enough; good, sincere people, but no matter how anarchy might have applied in the nineteenth century, if it did, it doesn't apply in a high technical society. It simply doesn't work. There was a big mess and a group calling themselves the Elitists took over. They're just what they call themselves. It's a dictatorship and from what little we know about it, not a very pleasant one."

"If any dictatorships are," Rex murmured. "I

never expected that instutition to spread into space."

The young black looked at him. "Why not, sir?"

"Don't call me sir, damn it, you make me feel old—and I am," Rex said grumpily. "Because the big requirement to become a space colonist has been, from the first, that your minimum I.Q. is 130. That and the requirement that you have a high Ability Quotient, a good education and be in all but perfect health. And I submit that few people with an I.Q. of over 130 would be silly enough to submit to dictatorship. How in the name of Zen did this elitist gang ever put it over?"

King gave him a cryptic glance and hesitated for a moment before answering. Then he said, "We're not sure. As I said, we have a loose federation of the asteroid belt Islands but one of the very basic understandings is that each member Island refrains from interference with the internal affairs of any of the other Islands."

"That makes sense if all of your communities have different socioeconomic systems, or religions and ways of life."

"Yes. It's the only way. At any rate, the anarchist system in Elysium simply wasn't working at all and I suppose that gave the Elitists their opportunity. At any rate, once again, the rest of us woke up one day to find a new regime in control of Elysium."

"And then what did you do?"

The younger man looked at him strangely again and said, "Nothing. As I said, our strongest tradition is that we don't interfere with the internal

affairs of other Islands. Some of the anarchists fled
and were accepted as refugees in the balance of the
Federation and, of course, they plan to return to
Elysium some day and overthrow the new tyrants,
but their chances seem remote."

"Why? If I know anything about anarchists at all,
they're the last type of people around who'd put up
with a dictatorship. Those would-be dictators are
going to wake up some morning and find their collective ass in a sling."

The younger man said, "Because the Elitists are
armed and the rest of the people of Elysium aren't;
that's why."

Rex stared at him. "Armed! In space? There are
no weapons in space except a few small caliber
hunting rifles for use in Islands where they have
game."

"They're armed with weapons up to and including machine guns and mortars. No heavy artillery,
of course. There'd be too much danger of piercing
the shell of the Island's cylinder."

Rex was still staring. He said, "Where'd they *get*
them?"

"We don't know."

The old man held a long moment of silence.
Finally, he said, "How did you find me out here?"

"Doctor Hawkins noticed that your fishing
equipment was gone when she got back to the
apartment from some committee meeting. She
told me this was your favorite fishing spot."

"Susie Hawkins, eh?" Rex looked at him for
another long moment before saying, "Son, you told
me that you were a tourist. Back before I retired, in

my profession we called that your cover. Why did you really come here to Grissom?"

The youngster released a faint smile that was three parts hope and one part challenge. "To consult the last of the private eyes," he said.

Chapter Two

Rex looked at his wrist chronometer, then picked up his fishing pole and came to his feet.

He said, "It's been a long time since I've heard that gag."

"Yes, sir. My father told me about it."

"Call me Rex. Susie and I are having a couple of people over for supper. I'll have to head back. Can you come too? Susie's a top-notch cook."

"Wizard. Dad wanted Doctor Hawkins in on it also. She's the one other person in Lagrangia he thoroughly trusts."

Rex's bike was leaning against a tree near that of his visitor. He went over to it, disassembled his fishing pole and attached it to the luggage rack. He went back to the bank of the stream and reached down and pulled up a string of half a dozen or so fish that average about a foot in length. He looked at them in satisfaction. "Supper," he remarked, returning to the bike again and putting his catch in the rack.

King swung his leg over his own bike, saying, "I don't believe I've seen that species before. Largely, we go for trout, salmon and bass in the Promised Land Islands."

"Speckled perch here," Rex told him. "When they first stocked Island Three, put in quite a wide variety of fish. Good idea. You get tired of just one type. We've even got trash-munching sturgeon. Best caviar I've ever tasted, not that I ate much of it Earthside. I was usually on Negative Income Tax. And up in the agricultural ring they've got one compartment devoted to lobster and crabs and still another to oysters and clams."

They started down the path, side by side, the rise steep enough that they could usually coast.

"Lobster!" King said. "I've never tasted lobster but I've read about it. I wonder if the Council has ever considered bringing them out to the asteroid belt. Probably they wouldn't survive the year-long trip."

"There ought to be some way to swing it," Rex said. "Look, uh, King, who sent you? That is, besides your father?"

"The Asteroid Federation Committee."

"Who are they? I didn't even know that your asteroid belt Islands had a federation until you mentioned it."

"It's a very informal organization with no real power. It's more an advisory thing. One representative from each Island. You see, it's the only thing that makes sense out there. Cooperation. All of the Islands have been built relatively close to each other; a few hundred miles apart, at most. The Federation has a mutual so-called coast guard for emergencies in space. And when a new colony is being established, such as Marx is now, everybody pitches in and helps, not only with technological know-how but with material things, tools and so forth. And then we trade a great deal. Each Island has its own specialties. For instance, Han and Ming grow sufficient tea for all of our Islands. We could, obviously, grow our own but the Chinese do it best. They have a score of varieties. When they first built their Islands they worked in the type of terraced hills that are best for tea culture. Pericles, on the other hand, has by far the best wine vintages. In fact, nobody else bothers to turn out wine, since theirs is so superior."

Rex looked over at him. "What do the Promised Land Islands specialize in?"

"Largely manufactures. Since we were the first in the asteroid belt, we've had the time to build a highly developed industry. We produce the most efficient tools, instruments, machines. A few things are still brought from Earthside or from here in Lagrangia, but not many. We're almost completely self-sufficient."

Rex said, "Wizard. So your Asteroid Federation has a committee, composed of one delegate from each Island, except for Elysium. Why did they send you to see me—and Susie?"

King took a deep breath and there was an almost apologetic tone in his voice. "Because we think the guns came from here."

The former private investigator stared over at him. They were beginning to enter the suburbs of

New Frisco and slowed their pace. There were other bicycles and pedestrians on the streets now and once they were passed by a small electro-steamer hovercar, a rarity in Grissom. New Frisco had a population of some 100,000 persons but powered vehicles were frowned upon.

"What guns?" Rex said.

"The ones in Elysium that I told you about."

The older man was exasperated. He said in irritation, "That doesn't make any sense at all. There are no guns in Lagrangia except for a few small-caliber hunting things, as I told you. What in the hell would we be doing with guns? The last time I saw anything heavier was some twenty-five years ago when a bunch of gunmen from Earthside came up in an attempt to sabotage this Island. They were representatives from oil interests and so forth."

"Where else could they have come from?"

They were pulling up before an apartment house. They dismounted and put their bikes in a bicycle rack before the building. The older man got his fishing tackle and catch of fish and they headed for the front door. The building was three stories high, and surrounded by extensive lawns and gardens. There seemed to be no lack of space in Grissom.

They entered and headed up the stairs.

Rex said, "In the old days, this was Professor George Casey's apartment."

"The father of the Lagrange Five Project," King said, nodding. "I've read about him. And, of course, Dad actually knew him."

"Yes, Casey's the one who was instrumental in

getting the Grand Council of Lagrangia to help your original colonists to build the Promised Land."

They reached the top floor and approached the door of one of the two apartments there. There were no locks in Grissom, nor even identity cards. Rex reached for the knob and opened up to let King precede him.

Doctor Susie Hawkins, as she was originally named, was seated in the extensive living room reading an old fashioned hardcover book, practically unknown in the asteroid belt whence King Ford hailed and not exactly prevalent in Lagrangia. Each Island had its own data banks containing, for all practical purposes, every book of every library on Earth. One read them in the screen of a standard library booster, connected to one's TV phone. King had never seen a real book until he had entered this room a couple of hours earlier in his search for Rex Bader. The late Professor Casey must have been a demon of a collector. The room was lined with bookshelves, well packed. It must have cost at least a small fortune to have brought them to Lagrangia from Earthside. And even to send a few volumes out to the asteroid belt would have been prohibitively expensive. King sighed. Some day, he'd love to read a real book, not one on a screen.

Susie said, "Wizard. I see that you found him."

"Couldn't have been easier, Doctor Hawkins," King smiled. "He was right where you'd said he'd be."

Rex growled, "These Islands are too damned small. A man can't escape from his women-folk."

He headed back for the kitchen with his catch of fish.

While he was gone, Susie said, "How is your father? It's been a long time but I remember him quite distinctly." She made a moue. "He didn't like white people. I don't remember whether or not I ever told him one of my grandparents was a creole."

He looked at her with amusement. "You are one of his favorite people. Frankly, I think he was in love with you."

Susie laughed. "He was a very handsome and very serious young man. I wish he had told me."

"Yes," he smiled. "But then I wouldn't be here, would I? And I like being here."

She laughed again at that and said, "Do sit down. Rex will be back in a minute."

In her late fifties, Susie F-E-O-67-MH2132 was still a handsome woman. In her day, she had been quite a beauty and though her hair was well streaked with gray now, she still had her original pert quality with laugh wrinkles at the side of her eyes and tucking in at her mouth. Age had lost for her some of the brisk, businesslike qualities that had characterized her in yesteryear.

King took a seat on a couch which faced the chair she was in.

Rex came back from the inner rooms of the apartment and went over to the small bar which sat in one corner. He said, "Drink, anybody? I could use one."

"A vermouth for me," Susie told him.

"Wizard," King said. "I've been in transit

almost a year and you know the taboo against guz-
zle in deep space. I'll have whatever you do. Just so
that it's very alcoholic.''

Rex brought the sweet vermouth to Susie and
handed a tall glass to the visitor. "Our version of
Scotch," he told the younger man. "For my taste,
it's better than the original Earthside stuff."

He seated himself in another of the room's ultra-
comfortable chairs, took a sip of the whiskey and
then looked accusingly at King. "Now then," he
said. "What's this about guns being shipped from
Lagrangia to the asteroid belt?"

"What!" Susie said, startled.

Rex looked over at her. "King tells me that he's
been sent all the way from the Promised Land
Islands by what he calls the Asteroid Federation
Committee to consult you and me. One of the
Islands out there, named Elysium, has been seized
by an outfit that calls itself the Elitists. They took
over power by force of arms and continue to wield
it, equipped with guns. At least, I assume that they
still wield it."

King said, "Yes. I'm in touch with the committee
by tight beam. If anything, the Elitists are more
strongly entrenched than before and the other
Islands are becoming alarmed."

"In what way?" Rex said.

The young man took back a slug of his drink. He
said, "As I told you, the Federation has more or less
ostracized Elysium since the take-over of the
Elitists. And that puts them in a spot. They need to
trade as badly as any of the rest of us. They need
many manufactured things from the Promised

Land Islands and the specialties of the other Islands."

"Such as tea from Han and wine from Pericles?" Rex said.

"Yes, of course, and many other things."

"But why the alarm?" Rex said.

"Don't you see? They're armed. We aren't. They're in a position to issue an ultimatum to the rest of us."

"Then, why haven't they?"

"We don't know. They seem to be waiting for something. However, they are building several spacecraft of a new design. Dad's of the opinion that they're of a military nature; space cruisers, I suppose you'd call them, and transports too. Perhaps they're waiting for still more weapons before making their move."

Susie put down her glass of wine in irritation and said, "But what's this about their armaments coming from Lagrangia?"

"Where else is there for them to come from?" King said reasonably. "Everything we import in the asteroid belt comes from Lagrangia, either manufactured here or Earthside." He looked from one of them to the other. "This is the terminal point from which all shipping to the asteroid belt originates."

Rex said, in irritation, "Why couldn't they have made them right there in Elysium? Heavy machine guns and mortars aren't as intricate as all that."

But the younger man shook his head and said, "They couldn't have done it without the knowledge of the original government. The anarchists might have been impractical but their industry was in control of anarcho-syndicalist unions and, like the industry of just about all of the Islands, the computers keep track of every nut and bolt. Now that the Elitists are in, I have no doubt that they can manufacture more armaments, but they couldn't have done it before."

Susie said definitely, "Well, they couldn't have been manufactured in Lagrangia. I'm a member of the Council here in Grissom and a member of the Grand Council of all Lagrangia as well. The same thing applies here as it did in Elysium before those so-called Elitists took over. It would be impossible to manufacture any such things as military weapons in our computerized industry without our knowledge."

The young black finished his drink. He said, "We don't believe that they originated here but simply that they were shipped from here to the asteroid belt."

"You think that they came up from Earthside, eh?" Rex said, looking thoughtful. "That makes a certain amount of sense. There are still a helluva lot of weapons on Earth." He eyed King questioningly. "But why Susie and me? What have we got to do with it?"

King said, "Dad was of the opinion that you two are the only Lagrangists we could be sure of."

Rex growled, "What in the hell is that supposed to mean? There are nearly three million Lagrangists."

The other seemed somewhat taken aback. "No more than that? But don't you see? Even though the armaments originated on Earth, there had to be somebody here, in Lagrangia, who made the arrangements to transship them to Elysium. And we haven't the slightest idea of just who it might have been. Or even whether or not the shipments are continuing under the supervision of this unknown person or persons. Obviously, the Asteroid Federation Committee had to trust someone whom we could initially contact, and my father recommended you two, especially since Doctor Hawkins . . ."

"Susie," she murmured. "We've dropped the use of academic degrees, since about half of all Lagrangists have doctorates."

". . . is on the Grand Council and, uh, Rex is an experienced private investigator."

"Look," Rex said impatiently. "Why don't your Federation people whomp up some weapons of your own? From what you've said about your highly developed industry in the Promised Land Islands alone, you could at least duplicate anything this Elysium gang has in no time flat."

The other looked at him wanly. "We considered that, but what you're suggesting would initiate the danger of war in space. An arms race and a cold war, always threatening to go hot. And do you realize the vulnerability of space Islands? Why, if the information in the data banks is valid, and of course it is, a cannon no larger than a French 75 of the First World War could shatter the largest of Islands with a few rounds."

"Yeah," Rex muttered in reluctant acceptance.

Susie said, "I'm still not quite clear why Whip

and his colleagues sent you, King. What did you,
with our assistance, expect to accomplish? It seems
to me that it's already too late, even if we could find
out who was guilty of making the transshipments.
At least two years have elapsed since it was done. At
the very least. The trip takes the better part of a
year, which means it took a year for the shipment to
get to the Elitists on Elysium and it took a year for
you to travel in to Lagrangia on your mission."

He nodded. "Because we're afraid that something's in the wind. We can't understand why, thus
far, the Elitists haven't issued an ultimatum to the
Federation demanding they be allowed to rejoin
and participate in the trade and other Federation
cooperation. Shortly before I took one of the
freighters that ply between the belt and Lagrangia,
five of the top Elitists left for here."

Rex looked over at Susie questioningly.

But she shook her head. "The automated space
freighters are going back and forth all the time,
bringing in raw materials from the asteroids and
taking back manufactures, delicacies and so forth
not available in the belt, from both Earthside and
Lagrangia. Most of the freighters have passenger
facilities, both to take new colonists out to the
asteroids and to bring back tourists and business
men destined for here or Earth. So there's no reason at all why King's five Elitists couldn't have
come."

"But why?" Rex said.

King thought he had the answer to that. "To
consult with somebody personally. They wouldn't
dare rely on even the most scrambled tightbeam.

Any radio messages can be intercepted. I imagine the equipment to do it could be made right here in Grissom, not to speak of the military Earthside."

It was then that the knock came at the door.

Chapter Three

"That'll be Virginia Dare and Balt." Rex said, coming to his feet. He looked at the other two. "I suggest that we keep this to ourselves until we've decided what to do."

"Wizard," King said, evidently inwardly pleased at Rex's seeming acceptance of the problem and the need for him and Susie to lend the requested helping hands.

Susie nodded at Rex's warning and said to King, as the former detective headed for the door, "You'll be interested to meet Virginia Dare. She was the first child born in Lagrangia. In Island One, of course, some thirty-five years ago."

"I'll be darned," King said. "That's a coincidence. I was the first child born in the asteroid belt." He stood and faced the door, preparatory to meeting the newcomers.

Susie said, in surprise, "Why, you look too old for that to be possible."

He grinned at her. "It would seem that we

mature early in space. But in actuality I was born in the construction shack that was used to build Promised Land One. My mother became pregnant on the trip out to the belt."

Rex returned with a stunningly attractive woman in her mid-thirties and a young man who seemed in his late teens.

The former detective made introductions. "Virginia Dare, Balt; meet our visitor from the asteroid belt, King Ford. He's doing the tourist bit, going back to the scene of his origins, Lagrangia and Earth. You're meeting space celebrities, King. Virginia Dare is the first child born in Lagrange Five and Balt is the first grandchild." He was smiling but then he frowned and said, "Aren't you, Balt?"

"As a matter of fact, I don't believe so," the teenager said. "I think some of mother's contemporaries anticipated her."

He shook hands with King briefly, as though it was an amenity he didn't particularly like.

Balt was a good-looking young fellow, which was practically a foregone conclusion, given his mother. But he had a somewhat petulant, if not superior, air. An expression denoting boredom, as though impatient of being amidst his intellectual inferiors. However, adolescence is widely accepted among the older. Young Balt had lots of time to discover that the intelligent do not necessarily inherit the earth; surprisingly, the meek often do. Most often, they're the ones who have it on the ball. Or, at least, if they're not meek, they project meekness. It's the

Lincolns, not the Nixons, who stand head and shoulders above the contemporaries.

Virginia Dare's smile was a glory. She was now a mature beauty going back to the British tradition. Very fine and light of complexion, light blond hair, blue of eye, perpetually smiling of mouth, gently classical of features. A quarter of a century earlier, Earthside, she would have been seized by the advertising agencies.

She said, "My; from the asteroid belt. We seldom have the opportunity to have social contact. Usually, you people are here on business, or the tourists among you almost immediately go Earthside. I'm afraid that the Lagrangist Islands are too similar to your own to be interesting."

Susie said, "King tells me that he's a celebrity, too. The first child born in the belt."

Balt said, looking at King, "Is that so? A black?"

"Afraid so," King told him. "Didn't you know that the Promised Land, the first of the asteroid belt Islands, was colonized solely by those of African descent?"

The teenager managed to refrain from completely yawning. "I suppose I did read that somewhere," he said. "Tell me, do you have the same I.Q. requirements as we do here in Lagrangia before one can become a colonist?"

King grinned at him. "Yes," he said. "Would you like to take me on at three dimensional chess sometime?"

The young fellow's eyes narrowed infinitesimally. "Yes," he said. And then, offhand, as though in warning, "I'm third generation gifted, so far as I.Q. records go."

King still grinned. "So am I."

Susie said, "Come on, come on. Who wants a drink?" She appropriated the glasses of Rex and King and took them to the bar for refills.

"I could go for a rum and water," Virginia Dare said, finding a chair as did the others.

"Not for me," Balt said condescendingly. He took a small plastic box from an inner pocket, opened it and selected a white pill and popped it into his mouth. "Alcohol's a depressant," he announced. "Who wants to depress their thinking?"

His mother looked somewhat worriedly at him and said, "Is that trank again, dear?"

"That's right," he said. "A stimulant."

King took his fresh drink from Susie and said, "Well, stimulants come and stimulants go, but alcohol's been with us since prehistory." He looked over at Balt and grinned his soft grin again and said, "Probably discovered by an African."

The teenager frowned at him. "I didn't know that."

"Most likely, beer was first brewed in Egypt, though some argue for Mesopotamia. It preceded wine by centuries."

Rex looked over at Balt and said, "What's this third generation gifted bit?"

Balt said airily, "I think we're beginning to breed true. Homo superior, you might say."

Susie had served all and now returned to her seat.

"What in the name of Zen are you talking about, young man?"

Balt wasn't one to dodge the limelight. He said, "I'm as good an example as any, I suppose. I had four grandparents, all born Earthside, all with I.Q.s of over 130, or they couldn't have become Lagrangists. I had two parents, one born Earthside, with an I.Q. of over 130, or he, too, couldn't have become a Lagrangist, and Mother was born in Lagrangia with an I.Q. of 142."

Virginia Dare looked at him in amusement. "How did you know that, Balt? I didn't."

"I looked it up," he told her. "And here I am, with one of 153. Third generation."

"What's this gifted stuff?" Rex repeated.

Balt looked at him condescendingly. "When they originated the Intelligent Quotient tests Earthside, most systems took 100 as average. From 100 to 200 was, simply, above average. From 120 to 130 was superior, from 130 to 140 was very superior and above 140 was gifted; in short, genius." He added, "When it was decided in the early days of the Lagrangia Five Project to hire only persons with an I.Q. of above 130 it was the best decision they ever made. And I'm convinced that it started the race on the road to becoming homo superior."

Virginia Dare scoffed, and said, "Dear, an intellectual snob is the worst kind."

The boy looked at her seriously. "But I'm serious. The second best decision the early Lagrangists made was to check the I.Q.s of all children who were born in Lagrangia at the age of ten. Those who failed to exceed 130 were returned to Earth."

"The parents, of course, perfectly free to return with them and take jobs with the project Earthside, if they so wished," Susie said softly. "But I was against that provision." She looked over at King and said, "How do you handle it? You, too, had the provision that each colonist, besides health and Ability Quotient requirements, have an I.Q. of a minimum of 130. What do you do when a child is born that doesn't make it?"

King said, less than happily, "We have a policy of *discouraging* them from having children. It's too far to return them to Earth, as you do. We don't *sterilize* them, but we bend every effort to discourage them from breeding."

Rex had kept quiet through this. As a young man, he had applied for a job with the Lagrange Five Project and had been rejected due to a less than sufficient Intelligence Quotient—barely. Only after his services to the project had the requirement been waived. He was the only Lagrangist with an I.Q. of less than 130—and, somehow, he had never had any children. The subject was sticky.

Susie shot a quick glance at him and said, "I'll put dinner on. It's my turn tonight, isn't it?"

But King wasn't quite through with the subject. He looked at Balt and said, "Do many of your generation feel the same away about this homo superior thing?"

"Most of them do. I guess it'll take a time to find out, probably when we start having children."

Susie snorted at that, before turning to head for the kitchen. "Three generations and you're going to start breeding true, eh? I'm a physicist, not a biologist, but my guess would be thirty generations would more likely be necessary, *if* we ever make the homo superior level."

Later, at the dinner table, after the fish course had been appreciated, Susie brought on the venison.

King's words were obviously more than mere flattery. "Holy Zen," he said. "This is really wizard. I've never tasted anything like it."

Susie said, "Oh, it's quite simple. I'll give you the recipe. It's called *Civet de Venaison Veneur.* You sponge the breast of a deer with a cloth wrung out in hot water and . . ."

King grinned ruefully at her and interrupted. "You've already left me," he said. "We don't have deer in the asteroid belt."

"I wasn't aware of that," Virginia Dare said. "Why not?"

King said, after thinking about it, "Well, for one thing, we don't really have the room in Island Two type colonies. And, for another, the distance is so great that transporting the larger animals presents its problems. However, the Federation has plans to convert one of the freighters to an animal transport, once we start building Island Three size colonies."

He looked over at Rex and said, "Didn't I read somewhere that when you get your Island Five finished you planned to even have a herd of buffalo? I can just see wrestling a buffalo calf up from Earthside." King laughed.

The four Lagrangists fell silent.

King caught it and looked around at them. "What's the matter? Did I say something?"

"That's the trouble," Rex told him sourly. "We're not going to finish Island Five, son. In fact, we're not even going to begin it."

The younger man gaped at him. "What do you mean?"

Balt said, in his irritating manner, "For that matter, there was no real reason for ever finishing Island Four. It's practically empty."

King's eyes went to Rex and Susie. "One of you mentioned earlier a total population of something like three million. I decided that you must mean here in Island Three alone."

"No," Virginia Dare said, toying with her venison, and keeping her eyes down. "The total population of Lagrangia, including Island One, the two Island Twos, Island Three, here, and Island Four is less than three million."

"But . . . well, I'm not up on this but I thought that Island Four would be capable of adequately supporting quite a few millions all on its own."

"It is," Susie said. "But there's nobody to populate it."

King shook his head dumbly. "This doesn't make any sense at all," he said. "Why, the whole space colonization program started here in Lagrangia. It's kind of like a geometric progression. Each Island, when it's completed, starts building another Island, usually larger. That was the original idea, the original dream."

Susie said wearily, "Yes, that *was* the dream— but it didn't materialize. When Professor Casey first conceived of the Lagrange Five Project he foresaw a day when the solar system would become filled with space colonies with billions, even trillions, of human beings. The project originally had several *raisons d'etre*. First, we were going to solve Earth's energy problems by building SPSs, Solar Power Satellites, and placing them in geosynchronous orbit about Earth, some 23,000 miles above the surface. The second problem the L5 Project would solve was that of the population explosion. Earth's population was doubling about every thirty-five years and room and resources were giving out. Then there were the scientific aspects. Telescopes, including radio telescopes, were fantastically more efficient in space, unhampered by Earth's atmosphere. And researching in zero-gravity had advantages in a hundred sciences. Manufacturing in zero-gravity also had its obvious advantages. On Earth, at least a third of your energy expended is utilized to fight gravity."

King was looking at her blankly. "But what went wrong?"

"Nothing went wrong," the beauteous Virginia Dare said softly. "The whole dream was realized within the span of my life, up to this point. The High Frontier dream has been realized."

King said blankly, "I'm missing something. How do you mean?"

Rex took over. "Look," he said. "The Europeans discovered the Americas about the year 1500. Some three hundred and fifty years later, the frontier was ended. Well, space colonization didn't take 350 years. As Virginia Dare, the first child in space, just told you: in the thirty-six years or so of her lifetime, all goals have been realized."

"This doesn't make any sense to me at all."

They had all stopped eating. Rex, Susie and Virginia Dare took up their wine glasses and swallowed, rejection in their faces. Obviously, the problem wasn't new to them and on the face of it, all were deeply affected.

Susie said, "Wizard. We solved the energy problem with our Solar Power Stations. And not too long afterward they solved it again, down Earthside, with nuclear fusion. It hasn't completely taken over as yet, more than half the energy currently being utilized Earthside is still solar in origin. But as they continue to build nuclear fusion power plants, their need for our SPSs falls off. We aren't building new ones. But the big thing was the population explosion. It stopped exploding. It seems as though man is losing his desire to have children. He's been losing it for a longer time than we realized back in the final decades of the twentieth century."

"Yeah," Balt said. "Good thing, too. Breeding a bunch of morons."

The older people ignored him.

Susie continued. "As far back as the late 1970s, five of the nations of West Europe *lost* population and even the United States and Japan were at the point where so few children were being born that the race was not duplicating itself. The original reasons for having children were gone. Large families had been needed in the past to work the farms or the factories in the early years of the industrial revolution. But now children no longer stayed at home and took care of their parents when they grew old.

Children were, if anything, a drain. You raised them, sent them through school, and then they moved off to almost anywhere to get jobs. Even in India they finally got the message. It wasn't the government's propaganda about planned families but the economic reality that children were a drain, not an advantage."

"And so it's been in space," Rex said. "Why bother to have children to populate the solar system? What's the percentage? In the old style nuclear family the husband worked and saw comparatively little of his children, but his wife raised them and devoted the best years of her life to them. By the time they were all grown and gone off, she was in her middle years. As the nuclear family began to break up and both husband and wife worked, neither of them saw much of their children, who were usually inadequately raised, a sizeable portion turning out to be juvenile delinquents. Why bother to have them?"

Virginia Dare added her bit. "And along came the generation gap and parents and children seldom any longer understood each other or even liked each other."

Rex tried to wind it up. He took another gulp of his wine and said bitterly, "So, here we are. The Lagrangists as a whole aren't inclined to have many children. If any. Susie here, for instance, has never had any. Virginia Dare's an only child. She in turn has had only one, Balt. Do you plan more?"

"No," Virginia Dare said thoughtfully—all but apologetically.

The old man looked at Balt. "How many do you plan on having?"

"Maybe one."

Rex said, a touch of sarcasm there, "That homo superior of yours isn't going to be very numerous."

King was still confused. He said, "But the earthworms, Earthsiders? Surely they still want to come up." He scowled. "Where in the name of Zen did that ridiculous term 'earthworms' originate?"

"It was originally used by one of the old time science fiction writers, Robert Heinlein, in *The Moon is a Harsh Mistress*," Balt told him.

Rex was shaking his head at the younger man. "No, evidently they don't want to emigrate out here. In the early days of the project, everybody and his cousin wanted to help colonize space. But that was when the world was a cesspool; pollution, depletion of the resources, decaying cities, despoiled countryside, the threat of wars, corrupt governments and all the rest of it. And that's where we slit our own throats. We gave them all but free energy, allowing them to mine the seas. We supplied them with raw materials both from Luna and now the asteroid belt. With our hundreds of thousands of top scientists and technicians we showed them the way to clean up the planet and often how to clean up their socioeconomic systems and governments. Earth is rapidly now becoming the beautiful planet she once was before the first industrial revolution. So why leave? Anybody with an I.Q. of 130 can make a very pleasant life for himself Earthside these days, and Lagrangia still has that double-edged requirement before you can come up."

Susie said, "Everybody seems to have lost their appetites. Let's go back to the living room and have coffee and brandy."

King Ford was obviously still on the bewildered side. After the spirits and coffee had been served, he took it up again, feeling his way as he spoke.

He said, "Those of us who went out into the asteroids are different from you pioneers at Lagrangia Five. You were scientists, engineers, technicians who were licking problems that applied to Earth, cheap solar power when the fossil fuels ran out, and the population explosion. We followed, but were motivated by ideological things. My people were blacks; some of the others were religious groups, and some had other socioeconomic factors working on them. Your present difficulties are understandable, you've licked all of your problems. Ours still go on."

"How do you mean, King?" Virginia Dare said, studying him with new interest.

"Well, take the Amish in their Island all of their own. What happens when some of the kids start studying comparative religion and wind up agnostics or even atheists? Earthside, such a kid just left the Amish farms and went to the city, or wherever, but what do you do in an Island? What do you do? You go off and build another Island of your own."

He thought about it for a moment and said, ruefully, "It even applies, in a different way, to the Promised Land. There's a tendency among the original colonists to divide up and go off to form their

own Islands. The 'Westernized' blacks, for instance,
as opposed to the Africans. Most American blacks
are racial mixtures, ranging in color up to and
including what they used to call 'high yallers' in
New Orleans, but the Africans are most usually full
blooded Bantus or Hamitics. They've got different
cultural backgrounds, too."

He looked at his wrist chronometer and came to
his feet, saying, "I really ought to get along and get
organized. I came directly here almost immediately."

"I'll see you to the door, King," the aged former
detective said. "Where are you staying?"

"At the so-called Lagrange Hilton," King told
him. "Somebody must have had a sense of humor
when they named it." He looked around. "It's been
a pleasure meeting and talking to you, though I
admit you've set me back on my heels. I'm beginning to wonder if this'll be the eventual fate of the
Asteroids Federation after the initial fervor has
fallen off."

They said the usual things on his departure.

At the door, King looked at the older man and
said, "Shall we get in touch in the morning?"

"Yes, of course, Susie and I will talk over your
problem. Frankly, I haven't the vaguest idea at this
point."

It was dark by the time King Ford reached the
street before the apartment house. He looked up
and across the cylinder which was Grissom and
could see the lights of various small towns and villages. He had read up on Island Three on his trip
from the asteroids and knew that New Frisco was

the largest city, with a population in the vicinity of 100,000; most of the rest of the people, amounting to about a million in all, lived in smaller communities, or in individual homes in the countryside.

Grissom was considerably larger than any Island in the Asteroid Federation and he liked all that he had seen thus far, including the people. Yes, even that conceited young brat, Balt. King suspected that he, himself, had probably been on the unbearable side at that age. The kid did seem to be intelligent, almost as smart as he thought he was.

King got a bike from the public rack and started off in the direction of the hotel. There were comparatively few people on the streets at this hour, but some. They strode along easily, without any of the frenetic rush that so often applied Earthside, if you could believe the Tri-Di shows that were sent up to the asteroid belt.

What the others had told him was disconcerting. In the lifetime of Virginia Dare, the first child in space, the Lagrange Five dream had been realized and was now deteriorating. Mind you, in only thirty-six years!

But then, of course, historically much can happen in thirty-six years. Suppose one took Earth of the peaceful spring of 1914. Thirty-six years later it would be 1950. Two World Wars had devastated the planet. Communism, Fascism and Nazism had all reared their heads and classical capitalism had reeled in the Great Depression; only in some countries had suitable adaptation taken place. The sciences had all been revolutionized. Airplanes, little more than toys in 1914, were now flying tens of thousands of middle-class citizens across the Atlantic and Pacific yearly. Television was taking over entertainment. The first spacecraft, the German V-2, had flown, and shortly the Sputniks would go into orbit. Nuclear fission had been developed, to the fears and hopes of man.

Yes, much could happen in human history in thirty-six years. And now, again, it had.

He put his bicycle in the ever-present public rack before the hotel and entered.

In actuality, the Lagrange Hilton was on the garish side, so far as King Ford was concerned. A little too lavish. He had found out only after registering that the place had been built in the old days for VIPs from Earthside, usually freeloaders on junkets back when the Reunited Nations had been in control of Lagrangia and before independence was declared. Professor George Casey and the other pioneers of the Lagrange Five Project had found it necessary to butter up the politicians and others among the power elite, if they wished to push their financial appropriations through. They must have been scornful, those dedicated, sincere, competent scientists and technicians.

The lobby was all but deserted at this time of evening. Largely tourists, King assumed, as he crossed to the elevators. There was no need to go to the reception desk, since there were no keys in Grissom, nor anywhere else in Lagrangia, so far as he knew. Crime was all but an unknown as it was in the Promised Land Islands. He assumed that what there was was in the hands of the Medical Function, as at home.

His small suite was on the third floor and he headed for it preoccupied, his mind still on the discussion with Rex Bader and the others.

He opened up to find the room dark, of course, and fumbled for the lights.

And the back of his skull seemingly caved in and bright lights flashed agonizingly before his eyes as he dropped to the floor, unconscious.

Chapter Four

Susie F-E-O-MH2132 parked her bike before the entrada of the Administration Building of Grissom and strode briskly for the door. On the way, she exchanged greetings with a score of other Lagrangists. Susie didn't know everybody in Lagrangia, all three million of them, but sometimes it seemed as though she did. As the Girl Friday, the right arm and Research Aide of the late Professor George Casey, she was possibly the most popular person in Lagrange Five and among the very earliest of the space pioneers. Indeed, though Earth born, she had spent the greater part of her life in the Islands.

She had lived for months at a time in the construction shack which had been towed out from Earth orbit to L5, there to begin the building of Island One with materials boosted up from the Luna base by mass driver. She, accompanying George Casey, had been the first to move into Island One, immediately after it had been pressurized but long before it had been completed. Upon the completion of Island Two, they had moved there. And on the completion of Island Three—Grissom and Komarov, the twin cylinders—she had moved to Grissom, still with the professor. Not long after his passing on, Island Four, as large as all the other Islands put together, had been completed but somehow she hadn't the heart to move again; Grissom had become home. Indeed, the seat of Lagrangian government remained in Grissom. It was the base not only of the Island Three Council but for the Grand Council as well, when occasion arose for the Councils of all Islands to convene.

She hurried up the steps to the entrada, passed on through and briskly transitted the lobby to the stairs, still calling out greetings and occasionally a few words to closer friends. It came back to her the first time she had brought Rex Bader here, some twenty-five years before. He had been surprised that the building, though its six stories were the highest in New Frisco, had no elevator and she had told him that it was deliberate. The Lagrangists took every opportunity to exercise and to avoid the ever-present automation. They didn't wish to become slaves of machines. Which was also the reason for the ever-present bicycle, instead of powered vehicles.

But now she realized that her pace was beginning to slow. Six flights of stairs were becoming six *long* flights of stairs. She wondered who, on the Council, would first suggest an elevator. The Conference Room was on floor six and some of the members were clearly getting older.

She entered the Conference Room to find that all

twenty of the other Councilors were already present, some seated at the heavy metal table, some
standing around in small groups chatting.

Werner M-E-O-70-RT7667, Councilor from the
Medical Function, looked up from the table, smiled
and said, "Ah, our Council member without portfo-
lio." He was a small man, natty and brisk, and
affected a small mustache in an era when facial hair
was seldom seen.

Susie said, "Am I late? Sorry," and seated herself
at the table next to the doctor.

As a matter of fact, she often didn't attend meetings, not being the head of a function herself. The
Council, the government of Grissom, was a planning body of scientists and technicians, not a group
of politicians. Each necessary field of endeavor was
represented by one democratically elected
Councilor. Rex Bader had once described it as an
up-dated example of 19th century syndicalism,
somewhat to the surprise of the Councilors who had
thought the Lagrangist form of government had
been their invention as the most sensible system of
running the Islands.

Susie was more of an honorary member than
anything else and although she had the right to
vote, she seldom exercised it. Today, however, several items were on the agenda that interested her in
particular.

The Councilors broke up their informal talk,
drifted to the table, and seated themselves.

Li F-I/1-A-95-AB9132, a tiny young Chinese
woman of about thirty who represented Entertainment, said, "I'll nominate Forrest for chairman."

Everyone either said, "Wizard," or "Okay," or merely grunted acceptance of that and Forrest M-E-O-75-TH6745 took his place at the end of the table. He represented Communications in the Council, was a man of about fifty, trim of build and, like all the rest present, looked to be extremely competent.

He said, "If there's no objection, we might as well first take up the requests of the committee from the retirees."

"And get it over with," Bert M-Il-A-95-JE2173 growled. "Damn Earthworms."

The retirees were not actually Lagrangists and had no voice in Lagrange Five affairs. They were tolerated and one of the requirements of their being accepted in the Islands was that they be beyond childbearing years. They chose the Island in which to retire for various reasons including the economy of living and the healthful qualities. Disease was all but unknown in Lagrangia, the climate was perfect, the air and water uncontaminated, and particularly those with heart ailments were able to live in partial gravity, up toward the axis of a cylinder.

They were tolerated because the income derived from their presence helped support the economy of Lagrange Five which still depended on some items from Earthside.

Forrest said, "Briefly, the retiree committee wishes us to recommend to the Grand Council that we convert what amounts to the whole of Island Four to one great resort to accommodate a much larger number of retirees from Earthside. In general, lakes would be made larger, beaches expanded, more sports suitable for retirees inaugurated. That sort of thing. They contend that it would lead to literally millions of the elderly coming to Lagrange Five."

"Yes," Bert said. "And we Lagrangists would be relegated to the position of servants to a bunch of low I.Q. earthworms. You can automate just about all of our functions except those involved in personal service. Hundreds of thousands of us would have to move to Island Four to wait on them. We didn't build Lagrangia with that in mind."

Werner said mildly, "Well, it would solve two of our pressing problems. One, it would give our unemployed something to do, now that we're no longer building either new Solar Power Stations, nor new Islands. And, two, as our sales of power to Earth fall off we'll need other sources of income."

Paul M-E-O-85-UE2227, of Agriculture, said, "No. Bert's right. Besides, if we allowed the retirees to multiply in number in this manner, in time they would demand more representation. In time, they might even find some manner in which to take over Lagrangia."

No one else seemed to have additional opinions and Forrest called for a vote. The request of the retiree committee was unanimously turned down.

Forrest said, "If there's no objection, I suggest we discuss the matter of unemployment."

There was none.

"And high time we discussed it," Evelyn F-E-A-90-TR4546, of Art, said.

Forrest went on. "When the Lagrange Five Project was first begun there was no such thing as unemployment. Everyone we hired, Earthside, was put to work and there was certainly plenty of it. Later, when children born in the Islands came of age, there was still a labor shortage, rather than an overabundance. But that was when we were still feverishly building new and larger Islands, and as many SPSs as we could. It was also before automation and computerization became as highly sophisticated as it is now. Today, practically all of the work needed to produce our needs is automated. And as a result, some ninety-five percent of our people are unemployed."

"Ninety-six point three, to be exact," Jean F-I/1-O-96-HH8821, of Statistics, said.

Susie looked at her. "I didn't know it was that bad."

"And getting worse," Jean said glumly.

Werner said, "And there're some ramifications that probably never occured to us in the old days. In the past, it was assumed that when man finally could produce an abundance with a minimum of actual labor he would have leisure on his hands and turn to the arts and to the sciences. But that's not the way it worked out. Oh, some apply themselves, but, unfortunately, the majority of our unemployed did not have the inspiration to go into painting, writing, the composition of music, or even handicrafts, nor the intellectual curiosity to go into the sciences. It is the exceptional people who do, not the average, even given the opportunity. Most are inclined, rather, to lead the hedonistic life. I might also point out as Councilor from the Medical Function that alcoholism, practically unknown in

Lagrangia as recently as a decade ago, is growing geometrically."

Jean put in, "So is the use of trank, particularly among the young people."

"We could ban it," Bert said.

"They would just find something else," Werner told him. "Man always does when seeking his flight from reality."

Forrest said, "Our problem, then, is how to restore the work ethic, how to reemploy our Lagrangists."

"With a strong hand," Bert said. He was one of the younger men present, about thirty, and had been born on Island One. He represented Transportation on the Council and looked as though he could supply the strong hand he was calling for. He was tough, solidly built, aggressive of mien. Handsome in the Scottish tradition, it was obvious that he would have attained the top in any society.

All eyes went to him.

He said, "Something has to be done to keep the Lagrangists from going effete. It's happened before. Man must be forced into his progress. The Egyptians had to be forced into building the pyramids, the serfs of the Dark Ages into building the cathedrals. The Acropolis, Parthenon and all, would never have been built had it been left to well-to-do free men, such as the Athenian citizens."

Forrest said mildly, "Since we seem to be using edifices for examples, how did the Empire State Building ever get up?"

Bert came to his feet and began pacing the Conference Room floor in agitation, trying to drive home his beliefs.

He said, "Those who worked on it were driven by the need to earn their wages. Did you labor under the illusion that they who must work for wages to support themselves and their families are free? No man is free who is dependent upon another for his food, clothing and shelter."

Susie said, "Those New York construction workers weren't exactly starving to death."

"Which is beside the point," he told her. "Thomas Jefferson's slaves were well fed, adequately clothed and housed. When they became ill, they were treated by the best doctors available. If one showed aptitude, he was educated. When one became elderly, he was taken care of. Jefferson would do anything for those blacks of his—except get off their backs. No matter how well off and secure they were, they weren't free and neither were those wage workers who built the Empire State Building."

Forrest frowned at the younger man and said, "What is the point you're getting to, Bert?"

"Don't misunderstand. I'm not opposed to how Jefferson lived, nor the fact that in order to have the free time in which to work and to make his great accomplishments he utilized slaves, the labor force of his time. Living under those conditions, the contributions he made to human progress are inspiring. The slaves, the serfs and wage workers were all needed in their eras if the necessary work was to be accomplished. Today, we are stagnating. There is no such class to push through the dreams of their betters. We have reached a point where science, technology, computerization, automation, have produced an absolute abundance for everyone, not only here in Lagrangia and in the asteroid Islands, but on Earth as well. And we stagnate. A strong hand is needed to put humanity back on the road to progress."

"Oh, it is, eh?" Werner said briskly. "And you're willing to supply it?"

Bert came to a halt in his pacing and scowled at the other. "Yes," he said.

Forrest shook his head in rejection and said, "Unfortunately for your ideas, Bert, our institutions here in Lagrangia are democratic. I doubt very much that our people would put up with being forced into projects such as building pyramids or cathedrals which we most certainly don't need. Does anyone else have any ideas on this problem of unemployment and the deterioration of the morale of the Lagrangists?"

Nobody else seemed to. Bert, in somewhat of a huff, slumped back into his chair. Susie looked at him thoughtfully.

Forrest said, "Our next question deals with the population. Our birthrate has fallen off drastically and even colonists from Earthside are not coming up fast enough to make much difference. Island Four simply sits there, devoid of all but a handful of Lagrangists who prefer solitude—the Daniel Boone type."

Li said, "We could lower the immigration requirements. Say to 125 so far as I.Q. is concerned.

That should make millions of more Earthlings eligible to come up."

Bert looked at the young Chinese woman in disgust. "If we lowered it once, we might do it again, and before you knew it the whole original idea of stiff colonization requirements would be gone and the average Lagrangists would be no different from the earthworms."

Most of those about the table seemed in agreement with him.

Werner said slowly, "There have been some great breakthroughs in genetics this past couple of decades. The so-called test tube superchild is an example. We could raise our children to order, in suitable surroundings; educate them thoroughly. In short, create our own ideal colonists without the need of going through the aspects of parenthood that so many reject these days."

"Holy Zen!" Susie muttered in protest.

"Why go to the bother?" Jean said. "What's the point in creating more people? If the population falls off, why not let it fall?"

There was irritation in her voice. She was an unfortunately plain woman, and obviously was well aware of the fact.

"What you're saying," Forrest said, "is, why is man? And why should he go into space? An eschatological question."

"A what?" Bert said.

"Eschatology," Lonzo M-E-A-75-KK1536 said. He represented Education. "A study or science dealing with the ultimate destiny or purpose of mankind and the world."

Susie said softly, "What is the purpose of man? Perhaps we don't know *yet*. Perhaps we are too immature to know *yet*. Perhaps we'll never know. Perhaps, even, there is no purpose. Meanwhile, we must do what we must do."

Chapter Five

Theodor Karadja took the small laser pistol the other offered him, checked it and dropped it into a jacket pocket.

He said, curious: "How did you smuggle this up from Earth? They assured me, in Moscow, that customs examinations were so rigid that it would be impossible for me to get through with a weapon."

Vadim Shvets said, "We made it here, Comrade Major. Comrade Pogodin works in a machine shop. It was not overly difficult to secure the needed materials and assemble it. We, too, are so armed."

"I see. How good is your cover here?"

"It is excellent, Comrade Major," the other told him. "I had little difficulty in securing permission to come as a colonist to Lagrangia, with my forged documents proving I met all requirements. I am an electrical engineer, at present unemployed as a result of the Council discontinuing the plans to build Island Five. My cover name is Stanley M-E-A-99-GR2398. That means that I am a male,

born on Earth, blood type A, born in 1999. The rest
is an identification number."

"I see. Very well, I have noted the other information you have given me. Make yourself immediately
available. Remain in your quarters at all times. See
that Comrade Pogodin does so as well. Have him
find an excuse to remain away from his job. Perhaps a vacation, or something. Where do you live?"

"In a small town named Heidi about three miles
up into the mountains. It has a Swiss mountain village motif."

"That's too far. Where does Pogodin live?"

"About one mile out, in a small isolated house."

"Alone?"

"No. He lives with a young woman."

"Is she a Party member?"

"No. She has no idea that Frol is a member of the
Party."

Major Karadja was irritated. "Have him find
some excuse to move her out. Let him quarrel with
her, or something. Then you move in. I want you
both immediately available if necessary. And both
have your weapons on hand."

"Yes, Comrade Major."

Karadja said, "That will be all. I'll call you on
your transceiver when necessary."

When the underling agent was gone, Major
Theodor Karadja brought forth the homemade
laser pistol again and examined it more carefully.
He'd have to take it into the countryside somewhere and check it out.

The major, somewhere in his thirties, was a
handsome man in the Latin way. He was usually

taken for French, rather than Rumanian, and, indeed, spoke that language as well as he did his own, the two tongues being related. He was tall, slim and moved with almost a woman's grace—or a panther's. He was dark of hair and eye, smiling of generous mouth on social occasions. One would have never, but *never*, have taken him for a top agent of the *Chrezvychainaya Komissaya*, once known as the Cheka and which had supposedly disappeared long years ago but hadn't, although its duties had evolved.

He had been irritated by some of the information Vadim Shvets had given him. Originally, there had been four agents here in Island Three, the most crucial of the Lagrange Five Islands. One had attempted to defect and Shvets and Pogodin had been ordered, from headquarters in Moscow, to liquidate him. The other agent had simply disappeared and couldn't be found. Shvets had been of the opinion that he too had defected and had possibly left on one of the automated freighters for the asteroid belt to seek asylum there.

Karadja had no idea of what agents might be on hand in the asteroid Islands. What irritated him was the fact that the ministry would send to Lagrangia the type of men who would even dream of deserting the fatherland of the proletariat. Were they idiots? Here he was on a major operation, probably the most important of his career, and he had no idea of how much assistance he might need before it was successfully concluded. The more manpower available, the better, when the crisis came.

He returned the gun to his pocket and swept the room with his eyes. It irritated him again that the room couldn't be locked; however, it wasn't of too much importance. There was nothing in the luggage he had brought up from Earthside to indicate his real nature. His cover was that of a tourist and the local authorities would have their work cut out proving otherwise, though from what Shvets had said there were precious little in the way of authorities up here. That had astonished Theodor Karadja. No security forces, no police, no courts, in the ordinary sense of the word; and, it would seem, no jails.

He hadn't been quite able to believe it. His junior agent's story had been that since no medium of exchange was utilized, crime in the old sense was just about impossible. There was nothing to steal, to gamble away from somebody, or to con them out of. The socioeconomic system was unbelievable to the Soviet Complex troubleshooter. As a youth, he had studied Marx and Engels, as required, but he had never quite believed that the system would ever evolve to the point where the slogan, *from each according to his abilities, to each according to his needs* would be feasible. But that was approximately what applied here in Lagrange Five, according to Shvets. Each Lagrangian was on what amounted to an unlimited expense account. He simply ordered whatever he wanted from the distribution centers, the restaurants, the bars, or wherever else one usually spent money or utilized his credit card. No record was kept of purchases, in a ruble and kopek sense of the word. It amounted to everything being free, which made no sense, though now that he thought about it, the Lagrangian system must have saved a great deal on bookkeeping, banking, insurance, sales forces and so on. Any good Marx-fearing communist could appreciate a system that largely dispensed with bankers and sales managers . . .

He left the suite, which was on the third floor of the Lagrange Hilton, and headed down in the elevator for the lobby and then the street. Shvets had told him that the hotel elevator was the only one in New Frisco, which was again surprising. Grissom was a strange combination of ultra-new and old-fashioned. For instance, the lack of motor vehicles in the streets and the utilization of public bicycles instead, as some European cities had done in the last century. The lack of signs, neon or otherwise. The lack of smaller shops on the city streets. Evidently, all buying was done in one gigantic underground ultra-market, by ordering at a delivery box into which the product purchased, if 'purchase' was the right word, was delivered automatically. If the product was too large, it was delivered by other means.

Before the hotel he paused a moment and looked up. He had only arrived the day before and this was his first visit to an Island. In his time, the major had visited some alien places on his native Earth but, on the face of it, nothing as alien as this. He wondered if with strong binoculars he could have seen, in the valleys above him, men and women walking around upside down. For certainly, with the Island's spin-synthesized gravity, they were doing exactly that.

And, high above, near the axis of the cylinder, he could see a pedal-plane. He had read about them in some of the tourist literature he had scanned on his way up from Earthside. The gravity was so near zero up there along the spin axis that one sport was the flying of small aircraft, their propellers powered by a bicycle-like arrangement. An exhausting sport on Earth, but quite practical here. He shook his head.

He selected a bike from the public rack and climbed onto it, wondering once again at the local institutions. The bicycles were public property and the racks were all over town. You simply took one, rode it as long as you wanted it, and then left it at the nearest rack. Obviously, the Lagrangists were far from property conscious. But then, he reasoned, if everyone in a town of 100,000 owned his own bicycle New Frisco would be overflowing with them.

Not even a tourist, such as he purported to be, had to pay to rent a bicycle. The Lagrangists probably figured it wasn't worth the bookkeeping. For his hotel bill or for restaurants and such, yes; he had to utilize his International Credit Card. The credit deductions were made into the Geneva, Switzerland account of Lagrangia. But there were a multitude of little things in Grissom that would have been charged on Earthside, but were 'on the house' here; entrance to the theatres and sports stadiums, for instance.

As he rode, he wondered vaguely why still more tourists didn't come to Lagrange Five. The big expense, of course, was the initial passage, though that was coming down drastically each year that passed and as spacecraft became more sophisticated. Once here, prices by Earthside standards were shockingly low. But that, he supposed, was reasonable. With practically free solar power and endless resources derived from the moon and the asteroids, manufactured goods were rock-bottom cheap. And agriculture? Given sunlight 24 hours a day, 365 days a year, and no pets or parasites, how could they fail to raise as many as four or five crops of perfect vegetables and fruits a year? Animal foods? The best stock available of the animals useful to man had been brought up and were being scientifically raised. The cow hadn't originally been included in the first Islands, due to its inefficiency as compared to the goat, pig, chicken and so forth; but now, the literature said, they had huge herds of both dairy and beef cattle in Island Four.

Following a small map of New Frisco, given to him at the reception desk of the hotel, he reached Science Center and paused for a moment to look out over what was seemingly a huge campus. Yes, the center of the sciences of Island Three resembled nothing so much as an ultra-modern Earthside university, and a large one at that.

He had read, once again, that the scientists residing in Komarov, the sister cylinder of Grissom, commuted daily to the Science Center here. The distance involved, some fifty miles, was nothing in space, less than half an hour at the speeds they were able to utilize.

There was a reception center and the Rumanian parked his bike long enough to go in and inquire as to the location of the physics building. The live receptionist at the desk, a pretty girl, gave him his directions smilingly. That too had surprised him. He had expected some automatic reception screen rather than a living person. The Lagrangists, with all their modern features, seemed to avoid automation every opportunity they could, particularly when it applied to human relations.

He got his bike again and pedalled to the Physics Building.

At the desk there he turned on his charm and said to the girl, "I would like to see Academician Konstantin Barzov."

She smiled at him and said, "You must be a visitor. We Lagrangists no longer use either titles or last names. Konstantin M-E-O-66-WE1976 has his offices at the end of that corridor, sir. Could I give him your name?"

"I'm afraid that he wouldn't know it," Theodor Karadja told her. "You see, I'm a journalist, up from Common Europe. However, my name is Pierre Cannes."

She did the things receptionists have done ever since there have been receptionists, then turned back to him and flashed her perfect teeth once more. "Right down that corridor, sir."

Major Karadja thanked her and followed directions. The hall was only moderately filled with strolling men and women. Most of them, he noted, were on the young side. But that was reasonable. Anyone born in Lagrangia would still be young, and those who had immigrated would also usually be the more adventurous types and adventure is the drug of youth, not of age, as a rule. He also noted, as he already had in the past two days, that the Lagrangists seemed to be on the leisurely side, at either work or play. He suspected that ulcers were on the rare list in Grissom.

There was no identity screen, nor even a bell on the door labeled simply Konstantin. He gave a gentle rap and then took the knob in hand and opened up.

Beyond was a nicely done office, obviously that of a scholar, complete with books and various instruments none of which Karadja recognized, save for the TV phone on the desk, and the library booster beside it. A large window opened onto a view of a considerable expanse of the greenest of lawn, with mountains in the background.

Behind the desk was a somewhat stoutish man of about sixty. His hair was thin and grayish, as was his beard, the first beard the major had seen in Lagrangia, and his eyes were bright blue. Karadja already knew that the eminent scientist was a Russian, and the other looked it.

Konstantin Barzov looked up at him pleasantly enough and said, "Won't you be seated, ummm, Monsieur Cannes? Frankly, I am somewhat surprised at your coming. I can't think of anything newsworthy that I have done in the past two years. My current project is a long term one and I am not ready to publish."

Theodor Karadja said evenly, as he took a chair, "I am not really a journalist, Comrade Barzov."

The other looked at him for a long expressionless

moment. Finally, he said, "I see. And I am no longer a member of the Party, my friend."

The espionage troubleshooter said, "Comrade Barzov, once a man has been a member of the, ah, inner circles of the Party it is difficult for him to resign. Especially if he had been a member of the Academy of Sciences and hence privy to scientific state secrets."

The academician's voice was as even as the other's. He was obviously not easily intimidated. He said, "Nevertheless, my friend, I am no longer a member of the Soviet Complex. I have become a Lagrangist. I so notified the Academy of Sciences when I resigned my membership."

The other breathed deeply and said, "As so many others before you."

"So I have heard."

"So you know! You are hand in glove with all the rest of these traitor defectors!"

"That is not quite the term, my friend," the older man told him. "You intimate that there is some sort of conspiracy, some sort of organized group attempting to subvert the Soviet Complex and the Party. It is not so. We do what we do as individuals. I have many colleagues who were once citizens of the Soviet Complex and we work together; however, we are not political. We are research scientists who have decided to remain indefinitely in Lagrangia and hence have become Lagrangian citizens."

"I don't believe it! It's too widely spread not for there to be some organization behind all these defections."

There was no answer to that. The twice Nobel Prize winner merely raised his eyebrows.

The espionage ace banged his fist on the desk and rasped, "Don't you see what's happening, Comrade? Practically every scientist and technician, practically every engineer, who is allowed to come to Lagrange Five defects and refuses to return. It's insupportable. What kind of a slap in the face is this to be given the home of the proletariat?"

"Why not stop letting us come?" the other said flatly.

The younger man glared at him. "The Soviet Complex is one of the two great science powers on Earth. It cannot afford to drop behind in the race. Many, if not most, of the sciences are better researched in space than on earth. We *must* be in on the breakthroughs originating here."

The Russian looked at the other for a long moment. He nodded finally and said, "Soviet science is not denied the breakthroughs originating in Lagrangia. Although we have renounced our Soviet citizenship, we continue to supply the land of our birth the same material we supply the rest of Earth. We are not sabotaging the Soviet Complex, we simply do not wish to return. We prefer it here. Though we do not discuss this matter to any extent among ourselves, I believe my colleagues are of the same belief I have just stated. We simply don't wish to return."

"Why not?"

The academician sighed. He said, "My friend, when I was your age on Earth I had few complaints about my own material way of life. I had prestige. I

won Nobel Prizes, for the glory of my country. I was
first a Candidate Member, and later Member, of the
Academy of Sciences. A physicist can go little further in enjoying the accolades of his fellow man.
However . . . in those days there were approximately one million scientists and highly rated technicians in the whole world. Of these, approximately
one half were working on weapons and related elements pertaining to armed conflict. Some among
us rebelled but most were motivated by economic
needs. We had to degrade ourselves if we were to
continue to work in our various fields. Can't you
understand why practically every scientist on
Earth would prefer to come to Lagrangia? Whether
or not you *can* understand, we come. And come.
And come. To escape what you have made of the
planet of our birth. We hold nothing against you,
certainly not as individuals, but we do not wish to
return."

"Traitors!"

The Russian shook his head, as though not knowing how to get through. He said, "Were you of the
opinion that this applied only to the Soviet Complex? Believe me, the brain-drain, as it has been
called, applies to all Earth, including the United
States of the Americas, your biggest supposed foe.
Any scientist, engineer, or technician. Any artist,
in any of the arts, for that matter, even such profes-
sionals as top chefs and top entertainers, was mag-
netically drawn to Lagrangia and sometimes the
asteroid Islands. The brain-drain goes on, though
admittedly not so fast now. People with brains are
tired of old Earth."

The espionage agent came to his feet, his lips white. "You have not heard the last of this, Comrade Barzov," he said coldly.

The older man sighed. "I am afraid you are proof that I have not," he admitted.

Chapter Six

When King Ford came to, it was to find that it was morning, and sun rays were streaming in the windows. The blow he had taken the night before must have left him unconscious for long hours, or perhaps he had gone from being knocked into a deep sleep, if that was possible.

He blinked at the bright light, groaned and began to sit up. And it was then that he realized someone was bending over him. His first reaction was to lash out but he caught himself in time as he realized it was Virginia Dare, the young woman he had met at Rex Bader's the night before.

Her eyes were wide in alarm. "Are you all right?" she said.

He sat up and put a hand to the back of his head. There was a sticky substance there; partially dried blood.

"I don't know," he growled. "I'm a little groggy. Help me to the bathroom, will you?"

She took his arm, aided him to his feet, and accompanied him to the bath. There he ran cold water and dipped a wash cloth into it.

"Here, I'll do that," she said, taking the rag and dabbing at the wound. "How in the world did you manage to do this?"

"I didn't," he growled. "Somebody did it for me."

She was unbelieving. "You mean that somebody hit you? But . . . but that's impossible."

"How and why do you think I'd come all the way to Grissom for the joy of hitting myself on the back of the head?" he demanded, wincing as she dabbed again. "Hell, I could do that at home. Let me assure you," he added, "that I don't."

When he'd been suitably cleaned up, they returned to the suite's living room and he sank into a chair.

She sat on a couch across from him and said, "But nothing like that ever happens in Grissom, or anywhere else in Lagrangia. Who could it possibly have been?"

"I didn't see him . . . or her," he said. "After leaving you people last night I came back here. Evidently, there was somebody in the room but before I got the lights turned on, I was clobbered." He looked over at her. "What in the name of Zen are you doing here?"

She said, "It occured to me that you were a stranger in Grissom and that possibly I could act as your guide. I'm not currently employed; practically nobody is in Lagrangia these days, and I have plenty of time on my hands. I came early, so that you wouldn't have already left the hotel, and when I arrived I noticed that the door was slightly ajar. I knocked and when there was no response, I came in. And there you were, on the floor."

He nodded and said, "Thanks for coming to the rescue."

"I didn't do anything special." She eyed him for a long moment and said finally, "See here, you're not just a tourist, are you? I had a premonition last night. Perhaps it was the way Susie and Rex acted toward you. As though when Balt and I came in, you had left off talking about whatever it was before we entered."

He was feeling better by the minute and took her in.

He couldn't believe that this young woman could be involved in the arms shipments to Elysium. It was simply out of the question. Besides, obviously she was a close friend of Rex Bader and Doctor Susie Hawkins. And she was young, not elderly as the former detective and former secretary of Professor Casey. If he was going to accomplish his task for the Asteroid Federation Committee he might find himself in need of someone more active and perhaps more knowledgeable of the current workings of Lagrangia.

He said, "Let me dial myself some fresh clothes, and then let's get some breakfast and I'll tell you about it."

He came to his feet and hesitated for a moment to see if he was still at all dizzy. For all he knew, he might have some sort of concussion. But no, all vertigo was gone. He made his way in the direction of the bedroom.

When he returned, in a new outfit, they went into the small dining alcove and Virginia Dare dialed breakfast, saying, "I haven't eaten either. You know, Uncle Rex is going to be furious. After you left, last night, he told me all about your father and how they'd become close friends."

"*Uncle* Rex?"

The center of the table sank down, to return with omelets, ham, toast and marmalade, coffee and cream. Virginia Dare served them both.

"Not my real uncle, of course. But when my mother died I was still quite young, so Aunt Susie and Uncle Rex sort of took over. They were wonderful."

So. The relationship between King's only two contacts and Virginia Dare were even closer than he had thought. He was sure he could trust the attractive young woman now.

As they ate, he told her the same story he'd told Rex and Susie the day before, her eyes becoming increasingly rounder as he progressed.

"But it all sounds so unreal," she said, when he had finished. "Shipments of weapons from Lagrangia to arm a gang of right-wing revolutionsts. And then the coming of five of these Elitists to Lagrangia for some purpose that couldn't possibly be benevolent. And now, you being attacked within hours after arriving."

"It's real enough," he said, his voice grim, and touching the back of his head gingerly.

"But what could they be up to?"

He looked disgusted. He said, "That's what I'm here to find out. That's why I got in touch with Rex. After all, he's a detective. Or was."

They'd finished with their food. Susie pushed their dishes and utensils back to the center of the table and they sank away into the bowels of the hotel to be recycled.

She said with sudden determination, "I'll help all I can. Whatever they came for it must affect Lagrangia as well as the asteroid belt. Perhaps we should have Aunt Susie take it up before the Council."

"What would we tell them?" King said. "Thus far, I have no proof that the arms shipments were made from Lagrangia. Perhaps they secured the weapons for the coup from elsewhere, though I can't imagine where. Besides, just possibly somebody on this Council of yours might belong to the ungodly."

"Oh, I wouldn't think so," she said, as they returned to the living room. "Let's go and see Uncle Rex."

"I was going anyway."

Something came to her and she took up her shoulderbag from where she had left it on the suite's small desk and brought forth her transceiver. She activated it and dialed.

"What are you doing?" he said.

"Calling my son."

The small TV screen of the device lit up and she said, "Balt, can you meet me over at Rex's and Susie's right away?"

From where he sat, he couldn't see the screen but he made out the small voice. "Wizard, mother."

Virginia Dare returned the pocket phone to her purse and turned back to King.

He scowled and said, "Why did you want Balt?"

"Don't you see? Rex and Susie are members of the older generation, the senior citizens. You and I are in-between. Balt represents the young adults. Between the three generations, we have a representative in all groups. He might be able to come up with something that wouldn't occur to us."

He nodded at that, not too happily, and said, "I don't like too many people in it at this stage of the game. But I suppose you're right. Shall we go?"

He was feeling quite normal by now and they made their way down to the street and got bikes.

On the way to the apartment, King looked over at her and said, "I thought that you didn't use last names in Lagrangia."

"We don't any more."

"Virginia Dare," he said, as if reminding her.

"Oh, those are my first names. Originally, my last name was Robbins. Haven't you ever heard of Virginia Dare? She was the first child to be born in the New World. That is, probably the first European child in Virginia. And since I was the first child to be born in space, my parents named me after her."

"You said your mother died. How about your father?"

"He was susceptible to Island fever, to space cafard, and had to be returned to Earth. I was only eleven or twelve. I chose to remain, since I knew only Lagrangia."

"You poor kid."

She shot a look over at him and smiled. "Oh, I would have done all right. I wasn't the only orphan in Lagrangia. The Medical and Education Functions would have raised me, even if Uncle Rex and Aunt Susie hadn't taken over. Aunt Susie is a wizard at handling just about everything, and Uncle Rex is a beautiful old bear of a man."

They pulled up before the apartment building of their destination, put their bikes in the rack and entered.

Rex was in the living room, seated at the desk and scowling into the screen of the TV phone.

He looked up at their entry and flicked off the phone. He frowned at the fact that they were together and after standard good mornings looked at King questioningly.

The younger man said, "I let Virginia Dare in on the whole story."

"Was that wise?"

King said, "I thought so. She came over this morning to offer her services as a guide and found me knocked out on the floor of my hotel suite. Evidently, somebody was in my rooms last night and slugged me. Virginia Dare smelled a rat, since prowlers aren't any more common in Lagrangia than they are in the Promised Land Islands, and I decided that she could be trusted and could possibly be of help."

"She probably can," Rex said, getting up from the desk and going over to a chair.

When the newcomers were also seated, he said, "I've located your five bully boys from Elysium, King."

"Already?"

"It wasn't much trouble. They're right here in Grissom, which isn't surprising since Island Three is the administrative center of all Lagrangia. They're staying at the Lagrange Hilton, the same hotel you're at, in suites AA and AB. That might be the answer to why you were knocked out. Were your things searched?"

King groaned and hit his forehead with his right fist. "I'm a dizzard. It didn't occur to me to look. But if there was any search, they didn't find anything. You know how little luggage you're allowed to take as a passenger on a space trip. But how could they have known I'd arrived and that I was at the Lagrange Hilton? I don't know anybody in Elysium, so they couldn't have recognized me in the lobby, or wherever."

Rex said, "I thought you said that when the Elitists took over, some of the original anarchists fled to the other asteroid Islands as refugees."

"Well, yes."

"Did any of them come to the Promised Land?"

"A handful. Some of the anarchists were blacks, so they chose our Islands for refuge."

Rex sighed and said, "You'd make a hell of a detective. I suggest, King, my boy, that you get on your tightbeam and call your father, and let him know that they've got a spy on your Islands."

"How can you be so sure?" Virginia Dare said.

The former private investigator looked over at

her and said, "Somebody in the Promised Land
Islands sent a message here informing somebody
that King was on his way. Which brings up another
thing."

But then the door opened and Balt came in. He
looked at the three older people questioningly.

His mother said, "Sit down, dear."

While the boy was getting located, King said to
Rex, "Virginia Dare suggested we recruit Balt as
well, as an ally among the young people."

"Recruit?" Balt said. He looked at his mother
but she held her peace for the moment.

"That might make sense at that," the former
detective nodded. "But let me finish. Your five
Elitists must have contacts here, including whoever
made the arms transshipments. If so, it's very likely
that they have similar viewpoints. In short, there's
probably an Elitist group or organization here in
Lagrangia. Which brings up still another likeli-
hood. Somebody, Earthside, had to originally
secure the weapons there. Somebody with enough
resources to procure them. That brings up the pos-
sibility that there is also an Elitist organization on
Earth."

"Holy Zen," King said. "You mean it's all one
group?"

"Possibly. But possibly it's three different organizations with fairly similar ideas, cooperating for
their mutual benefit."

"What's all this about Elitists?" Balt said,
scowling his puzzlement.

King went all through it again, winding up with
Virginia Dare's suggestion that Balt might help.

When King was through, Virginia Dare said, "By the looks of it, dear, Lagrangia might be in danger. If so, it's the duty of all of us to cooperate."

Balt had assimilated what had been said in silence. Now he said, "Possibly that new government in Elysium is the best thing. Anarchism didn't work. Perhaps the new government will. There was an old science fiction editor, John Campbell, who used to say that any socioeconomic system would work if headed by competent, dedicated people, but won't work if headed by incompetents. Both heaven and hell are despotisms."

"You and your old science fiction," his mother sighed.

King was shaking his head. "It isn't true. Some socioeconomic systems wouldn't work if Jesus was the prime minister and all his disciples were his cabinet."

"Name one," Balt said petulantly.

King thought for a minute before saying, "Well, take the Aztec confederation of three tribes in the Mexican Valley at the time the Spanish conquistadores arrived. It was a bastard culture that depended on raiding its neighbors for a large part of its economy. The trouble was, their civilization wasn't advanced enough to have discovered slavery as a socioeconomic system. So instead of putting their war captives to work, they sacrificed them to the gods. At the dedication of one pyramid to the war god they are on record as having torn the hearts out of some 22,000 captives. There was another shortcoming in their institutions. They

hadn't figured out how to assimilate a conquered
tribe into their own domains, as the Incas did in
South America. All they did was go out and clobber
their neighbors and rob them blind. Then the next
year, if tribute wasn't forthcoming, they went back
and clobbered them again. No question of making
the conquered people part of an Aztec empire. They
were kind of a king-sized mafia. The Spanish didn't
conquer them alone. They led a revolution against
them. They were a catalyst that united the neigh-
boring tribes and finished the hated Aztecs. At the
end, two of the confederated tribes even defected
and joined the attack on Tenochtitlan. No, no matter who you put in as war chief, he wouldn't have
done any better than Montezuma. The basic institutions were wrong."

Virginia Dare said gently, "Even if this Elitist
outfit does apply in Elysium, which seems unlikely,
it most certainly doesn't make sense in Lagrangia,
Balt. Our job is to oppose them."

Balt said, "I suppose so. Wizard; I'm in. What do
I do?"

Rex said, "If I'm right—that there's a bunch of
them here in Grissom—then they've got to show.
There is no such thing as a completely secret underground revolutionary organization. To recruit,
they've got to show. They've got to hold meetings,
give speeches, write pamphlets, possibly print a
newspaper, get into the mass media. And the bigger
they get, the more in the open they've got to
become. Possibly this local Elitist group is now
smallish, but they still have to recruit if they're ever

going to get big enough to take over. So, our first job is to locate them, find out everything we can about them, until we get enough information to hit them.''

Chapter Seven

When King Ford returned to the apartment of Rex and Susie that afternoon, it was to find that Susie had returned from a Council meeting she had attended that morning. On Rex's suggestion, King had gone back to the hotel to check his belongings on the off chance that something had been taken which might give a clue to the prowler's identity.

But he could find nothing missing. Obviously, his sole luggage bag had been searched by his assailant but nothing had been taken, although there were a few odds and ends of personal property that had value. For one, a rather enormous blue diamond which King's father had found on one of the smaller asteroids. There was no one in the Promised Land Islands competent to cut it, so that when King made his trip, which possibly might extend to Earth, he brought the stone along with the intention of possibly finding a jeweler in Amsterdam who could cut the gem adequately. His father had suggested that he then put the diamond on the market and deposit whatever amount was realized to the account of the Promised Land Islands in Switzerland. The asteroid belt still imported quite a bit in the way of expensive tools and machinery from Earthside, and the international credits would be welcome.

But the rough diamond hadn't been touched. On the face of it, the searcher had been looking for other things.

King had his lunch and then pedalled back to the apartment on the outskirts of New Frisco. He tried to muddle over in his mind developments to date but the difficulty was, he had precious little to muddle with. He hadn't the vaguest idea of where to begin ferreting out the purposes of the five from Elysium. He had made progress in securing the assistance of Rex and Susie, Virginia Dare and Balt, but they too, thus far, were in the dark.

As usual, he parked the bicycle in the bike rack and then mounted to the apartment. When he entered, Susie, surprise on her face, was at the TV phone on the desk.

She said to Rex, "It's for you. A scrambled tightbeam from Earthside."

He scowled as he came over to take the call. "Earthside, for me? At my age, I'm not even sure I still know anybody Earthside. It's been a long time. And why scrambled?"

She made way for him and he seated himself before the screen. On it was a face that he didn't recognize. A squarish face, a conservative face, a face that looked as though it had been in a barber's chair for the works, including massage, only moments before.

"It's your Yo-Yo," the elderly former detective said. "Start spinning it."

The other said briskly, "Dale Mickoff, Inter-American Bureau of Investigation."

"Mickoff?" Rex said, surprised.

"That's right. I understand you once knew my father."

"Yes, years ago. How is John?"

"Not too good. He's beginning to feel the years."

"So am I," Rex said grimly. "What's the purpose of this call? At these prices, I don't imagine you just want to chat over old times."

"No. It seems that Theodor Karadja is in Lagrangia."

"Never heard of him."

"A Rumanian agent of the *Chrezvychainaya Komissaya*, probably their best. Their top hatchet-man since Ilya Simonov was operating."

"I knew Simonov in the old days," Rex said. "But what's this what's-his-name doing in Lagrangia?"

"Theodor Karadja. We don't know. We had detectors on him and we're of the opinion that he wasn't aware of them. Some new models. We traced him to the shuttleport in Los Alamos and from there we know he took off for Lagrange Five. But you people don't cooperate with the IABI . . ."

"Nor any other Earthside police organizations," Rex put in.

"We have no manner of knowing where he's gone, in Lagrangia, or what he's up to."

Rex said, "Why tell me?"

"He's never utilized by his ministry for less than top priority assignments."

Rex repeated, "Why tell me?"

The other looked at him reprovingly. "You're the nearest thing to a policeman in Lagrangia." He smiled a sterile smile. "My father calls you the last of the private eyes."

Rex grunted. "He also used to call me the last of the gumshoes, the hawkshaws, the private peepers, the shamuses. Very jolly. But I've been retired a couple of decades or so. Do I look like a kid to be running around chasing top Soviet Complex operatives?"

Mickoff said, "We don't know what you can do with it, but we just thought we'd pass the information along. So far as we're concerned, if old Ted Karadja falls off one of your Islands, it couldn't happen to a nicer guy. By the way, his cover name is Pierre Cannes and he's supposedly a tourist."

The old man said, "I could pass on the information to the Council. That's the governing body up here."

"Yes, we know. But aren't some of them Russians, or others originally from the Soviet Complex?"

"Yes."

"Then it's possible that they'd tip him off. He's probably in touch with them."

"I doubt it," Rex said sourly. "But it's possible."

The IABI man said, "Well, we just thought we'd let you know. What you can do about it is up to you." He added, "Here's a picture of him."

His face faded and for a full minute was replaced with a portrait of Theodor Karadja. Then he was back again.

"Wizard," the older man said. "You've tipped me off. Thanks. Say hello to your old man for me."

The other's face softened in a frosty smile. With a cavalier's salute, he broke the connection.

Rex looked over at Susie and King who had been listening in.

"That's a complication," he said. "Just as sure as Zen made little green apples, it has something to do with the Elitists."

Susie said, "Why should the IABI tell us?"

"Because the cold war is supposedly over . . . but isn't. The IABI takes every opportunity to throw a monkey wrench into any KGB or any other Soviet Complex operators. Mickoff is hoping that we'll take some action that will get this Karadja's ass in a sling. They probably have a dossier on him as long as your arm."

King said, trying to be helpful, "Are there any other Party members up here?"

Susie looked at him and said, "Yes, and from way back. Lagrangia isn't political, so far as Earth is concerned. Some of our most prestigious colonists come from the Soviet Complex, including such outstanding scientists as Konstantin Barzov, as he was called back when he was winning Nobel Prizes. Like many members of the Academy of Sciences, he was a Party member, although I doubt if politics ever meant a great deal to him . . . if anything. It's something like Latin country scientists, say French and Italians, being Catholics. Few real scientists are religious, but sometimes they pay lip service for the sake of peace in the family, or because they're too lazy to get into the hassle of arguing religion, which isn't of any real interest to them."

King said, "Can we locate this Theodor Karadja? It might be some sort of a lead."

"No trouble at all," Rex told him. "He's going under the name Pierre Cannes. He'll be in the computer banks. He's probably staying at one of the hotels. By the way, are you heeled?"

"Heeled?"

"Are you carrying a gun?"

"I've never even seen one."

"Oh, wizard." The older man stood and went over to the bar. "Let's have a Zen-damned drink. The last of the private eyes, eh? I'm probably the only man in Lagrangia who's ever been shot at."

Susie said sweetly, "Don't be a male chauvinist pig."

Rex looked at her and laughed. He said, "Darling, I haven't heard that term in a quarter of a century. But excuse me. I'm probably the only *person* in Lagrangia who's ever been shot at. Now what do you want?"

"A vermouth," she said, grinning at him.

"Whiskey," King said. "That pseudo-whiskey you make up here."

Rex brought the drinks back to them. His face looked tired.

He reseated himself and said to King, "So you've never seen a gun in your life."

"In pictures, Tri-Di shows and so forth."

"They have nothing to do with real guns. Tri-Di

shows, I mean. Some asinine character unlimbers with an old time submachinegun and sprays about ten of the bad guys. They all fall over dead, as though each was hit in the head or heart. Nobody kicks, nobody threshes, nobody coughs up blood or splashes it around. They just fall dead, period. On the other hand, when one of the good guys gets hit, he has time to make with a last message, to mother, or 'the chief,' or whoever. Then he dies beautifully. Believe me, I have never seen anyone die beautifully as a result of being hit in a gun fight. Have you ever seen a chicken have its head cut off and flop around? That's more like the way we humans die in combat."

"Good heavens, Rex," Susie said.

"Yeah," the old man said. He stood and went over to a chest of drawers, opened one and stared down into it for a long moment.

He sighed and reached down and selected several items and returned with them to where the others sat. In his hands were two shoulder holsters and some cleaning equipment. He sat with a sigh and put the stuff on the cocktail table before him.

He brought forth a stubby looking gun, which was heavily greased, and said to King, "This is a 9mm Gyro-jet pistol, one of the most dangerous handguns ever devised, short of a laser, and they're supposedly out of circulation, banned by every government on Earth—supposedly."

He took up a soft cloth and began stripping the weapon and cleaning it.

He said, "A Gyro-jet launches a rocket slug rather than the standard gunpowder propelled bullet. The slug keeps accelerating past the gun barrel, and it'll stop anything on legs. If you shoot somebody with a Gyro-jet and hit him just any place at all and he doesn't fall down, you go around behind him to see what's holding him up."

"Good heavens, Rex," Susie said in protest. "I didn't know you had those in the apartment."

Rex continued to clean the gun. He said, "They're left over from the old days." He looked at King again. "One of them was mine back when I was a private detective and a bodyguard. The other one I took from a bad-o from Earthside who was trying to clip Professor Casey."

King was staring at the gun the older man was working on. He said, "But . . . but what . . ."

Rex said, "The party is evidently getting rough. If this Karadja is a top Soviet operative, like Mickoff said, he's undoubtedly heeled. How he smuggled a shooter into Grissom I wouldn't know, but I'd bet my left arm that he has one. So, from now on in, just to be on the safe side, we'll go heeled too."

King said, "But I told you. I've never even seen a gun before, not to speak of firing one. Besides, I don't think I could shoot a man even if I did know how to operate one of those vicious looking things."

Rex said wryly, "You'd be surprised how easy it is, if he's shooting at you at the same time."

The grease cleaned away, he reassembled the weapon, took up a box of the rocket shells, shook out a handful and picked up a magazine.

"This is how you load it," he said, slipping the ammunition into the magazine one by one. "Try it with that other clip."

His eyes staring in fascination, King obeyed orders.

Rex said, "You might as well load those other two clips too. We'll want spares."

He stood up and donned the shoulder holster rig, then picked up the cleaned gun and jacked a shell into the firing chamber, then flicked on the safety stud. He tucked the gun into the holster and drew it a couple of times to see if it was riding well and wouldn't stick. He put his jacket back on, resumed his seat, and calmly began to clean the second weapon.

He said, "No sane person wants to shoot anybody, but sometimes you can't avoid it. This Elitist group from Elysium took over power with force and violence. I assume that in so doing they finished off some of those poor ineffectual anarchists. So they're killers. And this Theodor Karadja; if he's the top hatchetman that Dale Mickoff says he is, he's probably wasted more people than malaria. So the party's getting rough, King. Do you want to pull out?"

"No," the younger man said, his voice low.

Rex finished cleaning the second gun and handed it over to the other. "Wizard," he said. "Put one of the magazines in the butt of your Gyro-jet, the way I did. As you do so, point the gun away from Susie and me, and down at the floor. Then feed a slug into the barrel. That little stud on the left of the gun is the safety. Flick it on. You've got to remember to flick it off again before the piece will fire."

King obeyed orders, albeit a bit clumsily.

Rex said, "Wizard. Now get into your rig."

"Look, Rex, this is completely beyond me. If I had to shoot, I'd probably blow my foot off."

The aged detective nodded and stood. "That's why we're going out into the wilderness to try a few shots."

Susie said, an element of desperation in her voice, "Rex . . ."

He looked at her sadly and interrupted. "The chips are down, Susie. It's been a long time but, once again, it looks as though the bets are down. If I had another gun, I'd give it to Balt."

"He's only a child!"

"In the old days, they used to draft people his age. Come on, King."

Down on the street, Rex and King got two bicycles and began retracing the route to the countryside which King had taken the day before in his search for the retired detective.

As they rode, Rex said, "Don't ever pull a gun unless you're willing and ready to use it. And if you pull it, don't hesitate. The cemeteries are full of men who hesitated. And don't try anything fancy, like aiming for an arm or leg. Aim for his belly. It's bigger."

Rex maintained silence for the balance of the ride. He led King well out of the suburbs of New Frisco and into the so-called wilderness and well away from any other bicyclists or hikers they saw. He obviously knew the area well. The dirt road became a path and then they took off on a smaller path that led deeper into woods.

King said, "Your trees are considerably larger here than they are in the Promised Land Islands."

The older man nodded. "They're beginning to cut some, for furniture and such items. There's something about metals or plastics—no matter how you try to disguise them, they aren't up to mahogany and spruce. Here we are."

They were in a small glen, nestled in a valley so that it was surrounded by hills. They put their bikes up against trees.

Rex said, "The Gyro-jet has a sort of whip-crack sound. Not too very loud. We shouldn't be heard. Even if we are, they'll think it's some hunter."

King nodded.

"Wizard," Rex said. "We'll try a little dry firing first. We don't have so much ammo that we can waste it. Give me your gun."

King produced the weapon and handed it over. Rex showed him first how to remove the clip of rocket slugs and dropped it into a side pocket. Then he showed him how to hold the gun, first single handed, then double, both standing and sitting. He went through the process of using a rest, such as the side of a tree, or the top of a boulder, if either were available. Then he demonstrated pulling the trigger and firing.

He said, "We're not going to be able to make a marksman of you. We don't have either the time or the ammo. We're going to have to be satisfied with what's known as close-quarter combat shooting. It's a matter of record that the average gun shooting fray takes place at a distance not exceeding twenty feet. Any distance not exceeding forty feet can be considered as close quarters in the combat use of a pistol. Beyond that distance, only trained marksmen are effective."

"These sights aren't very big," King said, concentrating.

"You're not going to be using the sights. You'll just point and fire."

"Okay."

"Now the best all-around method for combat firing without the aid of sights goes like this." The old man demonstrated. "The body is in a forward crouch, the feet in a natural position, permitting another step forward. To fire the weapon, the shooter grips the gun convulsively and with a straight locked wrist and elbow—the pivot point being the shoulder joint—raises the weapon from the ready position to the level with the eyes and fires. The gun should always be raised high enough so that, at the time the trigger is pulled, the gun is directly in the shooter's line of vision to the other guy. And don't pause before firing, once the gun's at eye level."

"Wizard," King said, trying to take it in. He still wasn't happy about guns, Gyro-jets or otherwise.

And it was then that something smashed into the tree next to them and immediately afterward a shot rang out.

"Down!" Rex yelled, falling himself. "Roll for that little gully."

King froze. Another shot reverberated. Rex, on the ground, lashed out with his feet and knocked the younger man sprawling.

"Roll," he snapped, clutching for his own gun.

King, completely confused, tried to obey orders. Somehow or other, he got to the gully.

Rex, behind a boulder he'd been using to demonstrate how to use a rest, whipped out two quick shots.

"Still got that gun?" he yelled over.

"Uh . . . uh, yes. I didn't know it, but I have. What . . . what should I do?"

"We're under fire. Somebody with a rifle. Keep down. He's up on that hill. Have you got that extra magazine we brought from the apartment?"

King fumbled in his jacket pocket. "Yes."

Another shot rang out, and its passage through the brush in their vicinity was noted.

"Load up, the way I showed you," Rex called.

The former detective fired once more.

"Stay down," he called over. "And keep the gun ready. There might be more of them."

King was panting, but he did as directed. He didn't even know from which direction the shots had come. He held the Gyro-jet clumsily, at the ready. But at gut-level, he understood something that the old man had said earlier, "*If he's shooting at you . . .*"

After long moments, the ex-detective called over, "Stay here," and then, evidently, he was gone, slipping through the trees.

King stayed, gun still at the ready. Suddenly he remembered and pushed the safety stud off.

It seemed an eternity of silence. There wasn't even the distant song of a bird. Everything was tomb-silent. Then something moved in the woods. He brought the gun up quickly.

A voice called, "Holy Zen, boy. Don't shoot *me*."

Rex stepped from the trees.

"Whoever the hell it was, is gone. Only one of them. And by the sound of it, armed with a high-velocity hunting rifle."

King stood, brushing dirt and twigs from his clothes. He was dismayed. He said, breathing deeply, "But what's it all about? Who'd want to hit me over the head in the hotel and search my things? And who'd want to try and shoot me out here?"

Rex looked at him and said slowly, "That's the funny thing, sonny. He wasn't trying to shoot you. He was shooting at me."

"You think it was this Karadja?"

"No," Rex told him. "If it had been, he would have hit me the first shot, and then probably have finished you off. From what Mickoff said, Karadja is a top pro. Top pros don't miss, not under these easy conditions. This was a comparative amateur, and probably nervous. Probably never shot at anybody before in his life. He was wasting shots all over the place."

"Thank Zen he was an amateur."

"Yeah," said Rex, and spat. "Deliver us from amateurs, boy; you never know what they'll do next."

Chapter Eight

Theodor Karadja propped his tightbeam communicator on the desk of his room and activated it.

When a face lit up the small screen, he said, "This is Karadja. I wish to communicate with the Minister, scrambled."

"Yes, Comrade Major." The face faded.

Shortly, a new face came on. Shaven of head, heavy of jowls, Minister Wladyslaw Kurancheva was a Party leader of the old school. In his sixties, he had been everywhere and back, and had clawed his way up into the Party hierarchy with a bulldog aggressiveness that belied his fat.

"Theodor," he grunted. "You are able to report so soon?"

"A preliminary report, Wladyslaw," the ace troubleshooter said. He was the only man in the ministry to call the other by his first name.

"Go on," his superior grumbled.

"The situation is even worse than the reports led us to believe. Nor is it just our top scientists. Tech-

nicians and engineers also became Lagrangists
with no intention of ever returning to Earth. Even
half of the ballet troupe sent up as entertainers and
to study the dance in one-quarter gravity. For that
matter, of the four agents we had stationed here,
two have defected."

The heavyset man's small eyes stared at him.
"But what motivates these people, Theodor! They
are the cream of our system. They have their every
want supplied these days. The Soviet Complex is no
longer poor, we have realized every dream that
Lenin and the Bolsheviks had in the days of the revolution."

His hatchetman said, "If I understand it, the scientists, in particular, object to working under the
aegis of the State. They wish to make their own
decisions on what to research, particularly
avoiding the military. In short, they want more
freedom. They seem to see Lagrangia as a paradise
for the research scientist. The most modern equipment is available, the equivalent of unlimited
funds, the presence of the most celebrated colleagues with whom to confer. So far as material
things are concerned, this doesn't particularly
count with most of them. However, the standards of
living here in Grissom are at least as high as anywhere on Earth."

Kurancheva glowered at him. "You sound as
though you've acquired some of this so-called
Lagrange Five dream yourself, Karadja."

But his agent shook his head. "No, Wladyslaw.
I'm a third generation Party member. For me, the

world revolution is the dream. Since I was a *Komsomol* I have had that dream."

"Very well, Theodor. I really had no doubts about you, of course. What do you now recommend?"

"First, a question. Has the liquidation of Academician Barzov been considered?"

"Yes, but given up."

"But if he holds restricted scientific matters . . ."

"So do hundreds of others among the scientists we have allowed to go to Lagrangia. We can't kill them all. It would be too obvious to the whole world. What do you recommend otherwise, Theodor?"

"That we go into the second phase of the assignment."

Even on the small screen, the oily sheen of the fat man's face could be made out. He wheezed. "Very well. Contact me immediately when there are developments. And remember, only Number One and myself know what you have been sent up to do. If you are exposed, and this matter is brought to the attention of the Reunited Nations, you will be discovered."

" In short, I'm expendable."

"Yes." The other's face faded.

Theodor Karadja deactivated the tightbeam communicator but looked at the now blank screen for a long empty moment. "I knew that from the first," he murmured.

He stood, brought forth his laser pistol and checked it. He tucked it back into the shoulder holster Vadim Shvets had supplied him with, then brought forth his transceiver and called that operative. He asked a few questions and then said, "Very well, you and Pogodin hold yourself at the ready. I'm going in to confront them."

He deactivated the pocket phone, returned it to his clothing, and headed for the door.

His destination was one floor below that on which he had his room. He took the stairs, rather than the elevators.

The floor below was devoted entirely to the larger suites the hotel boasted. At the end of the corridor were Suites AA and AB. Before them was stationed a brawny young man, nonchalantly leaning against the wall next to the door of Suite AA as though awaiting someone.

He looked up and frowned as the counter-espionage ace approached.

He said, frowning still, "You have the wrong place. You can't go in. An important conference is going on."

Karadja smiled at him. "I know," he said.

He stepped closer; even as the other's eyes began to widen, and he began to bring his hands up, the Rumanian brought the fingers of his right hand together in what resembled a spear head, rather than a fist, and drove them at full strength into the guard's solar plexus. The other's face exploded into shocked agony and he doubled forward. Karadja slugged him on the chin and the guard continued to fall forward.

The Soviet Complex agent shook his head and murmured, "Amateur."

He bent and slid his hands under the younger

man's armpits and dragged him across the hall to the door of the suite there. He knew the place was empty. Pogodin had checked it out earlier. He also knew that it wasn't locked. It couldn't be.

He opened up, hauled the unconscious guard inside, and dumped him on the floor of the living room. He looked down at the other thoughtfully for a moment and then kicked him in the temple. It was an old trick that he had been taught when he first joined the ministry. Even if his victim revived, he wouldn't remember what had happened; his head would be scrambled for days—if not forever.

Karadja went on into the bedroom and secured a "Do Not Disturb" sign and hung it on the doorknob of the suite as he left.

He crossed the hall, his breath not even quickened by his exertions, opened the door and stepped into the room beyond. He looked around at the eight men and two women who sat comfortably, drinks in hand or on convenient cocktail tables.

Theodor Karadja smiled and said in English, "Good afternoon, everyone." He was an accomplished linguist, but Interlingua was not one of his languages. However, he assumed that most, if not all, of these would have English.

Bert, Councilor of the Transportation Function, snapped, "Who in the hell are you? This is private."

Karadja turned his smile on him and said, "This is a conference between five members of the Elitists of Elysium and five from Lagrangia. My name is

Pierre Cannes and I'm an uninvited delegate coming to join the get-together."

"Like hell you are," one of the men blurted. "How did you get past that guard at the door?"

"It wasn't very difficult," the Soviet agent told him. "If that's the caliber of your rank and file, you're facing trouble."

Jean, Councilor of the Statistics Function, said flatly, "We don't need any uninvited delegates. Now get out. Or do you labor under the illusion that we can't put you out?"

"I doubt it," the newcomer said smoothly. A pistol suddenly materialized in his right hand. "Have any of you ever seen a laser gun before? Believe me, they are quite effective. I could go far toward cutting down this hotel with this one."

All ten of them were staring at him. He returned the vicious weapon to its holster with a practiced flick of his wrist and took a chair at an advantageous place where he could see them all, and smiled again.

He said to Jean, "Yes, you do need another delegate. You ten represent Elysium and Lagrangia. You need a delegate from Earth."

"We don't know what you're talking about," Lonzo, Education Councilor, said.

Karadja turned his eyes in that direction. "Then I'll tell you," he said. "I'm talking about the fact that the first phase of your attempt has been completed. I don't know which of you are from Elysium but not too long ago your group, utilizing weapons secretly shipped in from here in Lagrangia, seized power from the admittedly inept

anarchists who had built that Island in the asteroids. You have now come to Lagrangia to make
your next step, seizing control here. When that is
accomplished and there is no fear of Lagrangian
interference, your group in the asteroids will take
the next step and, threatening military action, will
take over domination of the whole Asteroid Federation."

Bert blurted, "How could you possibly know
that?"

The unwanted newcomer smiled lazily at him.
"Aren't any of you beginning to guess? I told you. I
too am a delegate. In short, I'm an Elitist from
Earth."

Bert said, "There're only a comparatively few
Elitists on Earth, and you aren't one of them."

"To the contrary," the other told him. "There are
quite a few of us. It's just that so far your groups
and mine haven't gotten together."

It was Jean who caught on. "He's from the Soviet
Complex," she said emptily.

Karadja smiled at her. "Which has been ruled by
an elite since 1917."

They assimilated that.

"What do you want?" one of the men said. He
was a dour looking type, somewhere in his mid-
fifties. "I'm Field Marshal Van Eckmann."

"Field Marshal?" the Rumanian said, smiling
still once again.

"In an Island armed with a few machine guns
and mortars?" He turned more serious. "What we
wish to do is cooperate with you. I represent Number One himself and have carte blanche."

"Cooperate how?" Bert blurted.

"In any way you might require. Obviously, our facilities are unlimited. You see, your Elitists wish to take over control of the Islands, both here in Lagrangia and in the asteroid belt. Our wish is to take over Earth. The cold war is on the verge of ending, at long last, and the Party is ready to take over world government."

"We Elitists will take over world government eventually," Bert said, agitation in his voice.

The Rumanian shook his head. "No. We are acquainted with the fact that that was your eventual plan. But no."

Lonzo said, "How do you know so much about our plans, Pierre Cannes, or whatever your real name is?"

Karadja looked over at him and said, "My dear sir, are you so naive that you think we didn't infiltrate your organizations when they first began? All of your plans are immediately forwarded to the ministry I represent. Our agents are even in your upper echelons."

"Someone here, for instance?" Jean said. She was obviously a quick thinker.

He smiled at her.

The self-named Field Marshal said, "Of just what would this cooperation consist?"

Theodor Karadja's face became more serious and he said, "I'll put my cards on the table, as the Americans have it. Some of our Soviet scientists and others who have come to Lagrangia Five have seen fit to sever their relations with the home country. When you come to power, we wish to resume control of them."

"Some!" Bert said, sneering. "Practically all of them."

The espionage ace didn't answer that, merely eyed the other.

The Field Marshal said dourly, "And what would we get out of this?"

"Our assistance in your coming to power. And also . . ." the Rumanian hesitated before adding, ". . . we would refrain from attacking Elysium."

All eyes were on him.

He said, looking at them one by one, "Surely you realize that both the Soviet Complex and the United States of the Americas have built several space cruisers, quite capable of the journey to the asteroid belt." He turned his eyes to the Field Marshal again. "They are not armed with heavy machine guns and mortars. They are armed with laser rifles and even nuclear weapons."

For a moment there was silence.

Then Bert said dangerously, "At the first signs of either the Soviet Complex or the United States interfering in the internal affairs of either Lagrangia or Elysium, we will end microwaving solar power down to the surface and Earth's economy will collapse."

The other shook his head. "You make two mistakes. First of all, the Satellite Solar Power Stations are not here in Lagrangia. They are in geosynchronous orbit some 22,300 miles above Earth. Any attempt on your part to discontinue their use would be met with force. But the other mistake is even more important. You see, the Soviet Complex did not put all of its energy eggs in one basket when the SPSs first began to be manufactured here in Lagrangia. Oh, we utilized some of the solar power, but not to the extent the West did. Instead, we concentrated more on nuclear fusion and continued to hold in the background our rich reserves of petroleum and natural gas. Even if the solar power was withdrawn, we could convert overnight."

They stared at him in frustration.

Finally, one of the five from Elysium said, "But what has all this got to do with the Earthside cold war ending and the Soviet Complex taking over? If you attempted to take over the West, it would precipitate a nuclear war."

The Soviet agent shook his head again in negation. He said, "No. You see, we have a plan that will completely collapse the economies of all the Western nations. The collapse will be so complete that the citizens of these countries will have no alternative but to apply for entrance into the Soviet Complex. No military action will take place. The 'attack,' if you can call it that, will be economic. They will be grateful when we take them in, not disgruntled."

Jean said skeptically, "What's this method of completely collapsing the economies of all the Western powers? Their economies are at least as strong as your own."

"At this stage, I won't tell you. But it has been well worked out and applying it will cast no suspicions on the Soviet Complex. However, it can't be applied until you Elitists have taken over here in Lagrangia."

Bert said suddenly, "How about a drink?"

"I thought you'd never ask," Theodor Karadja said, smiling. "Barrack, if you have it."

Chapter Nine

Balt looked over at the girl on the pillow next to him and said sleepily, "That was wizard. Where'd you learn that kind of upside down position?"

Martha F-13-O-09-AB1696 grinned at him. "From Tom."

"It's more like athletics, rather than sex," he said. "You seem to see more of Tom than you do of me, these days."

"Oh, no. I was just feeling kind of horny the other day and you weren't around."

She was a roly-poly girl of about sixteen, with dark red hair worn unfashionably long, bright green eyes, a sensuous mouth and a body to go with it. Possibly by the time she had acquired another ten years she'd go to the dumpy side but right now she was mouth-wateringly lush.

They were nude but she was wearing a wrist chronometer and now looked at it. "You know, Balt," she said, "if we don't cut this out you'll be late for the meeting."

"Wizard. Let's go." He swung his legs over the side of the bed and stood, reaching for the clothes he had flung carelessly over a chair an hour before.

She sat up on her own side of the bed and bent over to slip into her sandals. As she leaned forward, her ample breasts fell out from her body.

Balt said, "Did you ever hear about the old knock-knock jokes? Kind of a fad about half a century or so ago?"

"No."

"Well, I say, 'Knock, knock,' and you say. 'Who's there?' and I give some name and then you repeat the name and add, 'who?' All right, let's go. Knock, knock."

"Who's there?"

"Emerson."

"Emerson who?"

"Emerson nice tits you got there, baby."

She eyed him. "A truly repellant jest. Why do you bother to read all those old books?"

"It's too intellectual for you," he said grumpily.

As they dressed, she said, "What did you call the meeting for?"

"It's kind of an emergency," he told her. "There's a new organization called the Elitists, or something like that. They want to take over the government. In fact, one of their groups, up in the asteroid belt, already have taken over one of the Islands there."

"Take over the government?" she said blankly. "Well, why?"

"So they can run things the way they'd like to, I

suppose. Why does anybody ever take over a government?"

"I could never figure it out," she said.

He looked over at her as he drew his pants on. "Are you sure that you've got an I.Q. of over 150?"

"That's what they tell me, Balt. I never paid much attention."

He turned and said, "That's the trouble with I.Q. It measures your potential intelligence but not what you do with it. That's one of the things wrong with Lagrangia these days. The I.Q. keeps going up but the educational level is going down. Nobody gives a damn any more."

"If you say so," she yawned. "I could never bear school, myself."

"I'll be damned if I know why we ever let you into the club," he said.

She grinned at him. "Because I'm a good lay."

"That you are. Come on, let's go."

They issued forth from the small suburban house in which they had been pleasuring each other and walked toward the nearest bike rack.

He looked over at her and said, "Martha, do you like living in Lagrangia?"

"I don't know. I suppose so; I've never been anywhere else. Oh, I've been to the other Islands in Lagrange Five, but never Earthside or to the asteroids. I have a lot of fun."

"Most of it is in bed," he said. "That's the trouble with Lagrangia. Nobody's interested in anything except having fun."

"What else is there to be interested in?" she said, selecting a bike, mounting it and taking off.

He pedalled along beside her. "The future," he said.

She made a moue. "Those old science fiction books of yours again. Why should we worry about the future? What did the future ever do for us?"

He groaned at that.

She frowned and said, "You know, perhaps my father belongs to that elitist group you were talking about. Only they don't call it the Elitists."

"Oh? What do they call it?"

"The Sons of Liberty. He's belonged for ever so long. I think possibly mother does too or, at least, to the sister organization, The Daughters of Liberty. She goes to meetings with him."

He looked over at her again as they rode. "Did you ever go to one?"

"To a picnic they held up on the mountain once. But it was boring. All old farts. And then one of them had to get up and give a long, drawn-out speech."

"Oh? Is that so? What about?"

"I don't know. I never listen to speeches."

He was disgusted with her. He said, "Didn't you hear any of it at all?"

"Oh, it was something about Lagrangia going to the dogs and how the Sons and Daughters of Liberty were going to have to take over."

"He's right," he said grimly. "Here we are."

The one story building before which they stopped was set back away from the street, surrounded by lawn, tennis courts, a basketball court, croquet layout and a magnificent swimming pool.

They racked their bikes and approached the door.

Various other teenagers stood around in groups, talking, laughing, joking. Several of them called out to Balt and Martha as they came up.

On the door was a very small sign, *Young People's 150 Club.*

They went on through and down the hall to a large assembly room which was already quite full of boys and girls in Balt's age group.

There was a podium at one end of the hall and Balt and Martha went to it.

Jim M-163-A-08-AB1818 looked up at their approach and gave his head a little toss in a way of greeting. He was a tall, gawky boy, over six feet, with a prominent nose and prominent Adam's apple, and was Balt's best friend.

He said, "Hi, Balt. Hi, Martha. What spins?"

Balt said, "Kind of a crisis. Some cloddies are anticipating us. Let's get going."

Jim scowled at him but came to his feet and mounted the speaker's stand. There was a gavel there and he rapped for order and called out, "Let's all be seated. The president has a message."

They drifted into seats, including those who had been out on the lawn and who now entered, and looked up expectantly. There must have been several hundred of them, ranging in age from roughly fifteen to nineteen. They were bright, healthy looking types without exception.

Jim pounded again and said into the mike, "President Balt says we have a crisis on our hands. Since I know no more about it than that, I'll turn the podium over to him."

There was faint applause, as Balt took over.

"Fellow members of the 150 Club, it's come to your president's attention that a group of what in the old days would probably have been called right-wingers are planning to subvert the institutions of Lagrangia, as they already have those of the Island Elysium in the asteroid belt."

There was a buzz through the hall at that.

He smiled sardonically and said, "Of course, we have in mind the same thing but we've been biding our time until we were both older and until our ranks were more full. These people are into their scheme already."

Balt waited until his audience of young people had quieted down.

He went on, "The purpose of our organization is well known to us all. Before any of us here were born, it was decided by Professor George Casey and the other pioneers of the Lagrange Five Project that their basic idea was not to colonize space but to seed it. Nobody was allowed to become a Lagrangist if his I.Q. was less than 130; unless his health was all but perfect; unless his Ability Quotient was considerably above average; and unless he had a good education. The idea was to bring the cream of mankind into space and leave the dregs behind. Lagrangia did not want the unfit, the stupid, the lazy, the physically second rate. The plan succeeded."

He paused for a long moment before going on.

"But something else developed which we suspect that Professor Casey never considered. The Lagrangists, with their I.Q.s of over 130, refused to be dominated by an Earth whose population averaged only

100 I.Q. Independence was declared. But what the Father of the Lagrange Five Project didn't realize was that it made no more sense for Lagrangists with I.Q. of over 150 to be dominated by citizens with only 130 I.Q.s than it did that earthworms dominate Lagrangia."

He held another pregnant silence before adding simply, "And we of the new generations are rapidly growing in intelligence. It is already time, as we know, to consider our future and the need for us to take over."

"Hear, hear," somebody yelled.

Balt nodded. "The thing is, the basic trouble about the rule of an elite is that once a clique gets into power, by whatever means, often by armed force, it's up to them to decide just who the elite is. When the Nazis took over in Germany in the early 1930s, they immediately announced that their bunch of bully boys, street scum and incompetents were the elite who would have to rule Germany. This group of which I'm talking is in much the same position. There is no reason to believe they are an elite. *We are the elite!*"

The cheers came.

Somebody from the audience called out, "Who are these bastards?"

Balt said, "We're not sure but it's possible that here in Lagrangia they call themselves the Sons and Daughters of Liberty. It sounds possible. Groups attempting to seize power usually adorn themselves with high sounding patriotic and ideal-istic titles and phrases. It was an old time American politician, Huey Long, who once said, 'If Fascism ever comes to the United States, we won't call it Fascism, we'll call it Americanism."

Somebody called from the floor, "Samuel Johnson once said that patriotism is the last refuge of a scoundrel."

Somebody else called, "Oscar Wilde said that patriotism is the virtue of the vicious."

And still somebody else yelled, "George Bernard Shaw said that we'll never have a quiet world till you knock the patriotism out of the human race."

Balt held up his hands to quiet them. "All right; wizard," he said. "We're all proving how erudite we are. But the thing is, what are we going to do about these Sons of Liberty?"

Jim, who had been standing to one side a bit behind him, bobbed his Adam's apple and said, "President Balt, have you already come to any conclusions?"

Without looking at him, Balt said, "Yes! We've got to update our program to meet this new danger. We've got to immediately begin to prepare. First of all, I suggest that we send emissaries to our fellow 150 Clubs in all of the other Lagrange Five Islands to let them know the situation. These Sons of Liberty are undoubtedly organized throughout Lagrangia. Then we must prepare ourselves for the eventual confrontation."

"How?" somebody called out.

Balt said, "I suggest that we form a new club, actually just as secret as the Young People's 150 Club. It could be called the Young People's Hunting Club. As an organization interested in hunting, we will be eligible to acquire hunting rifles and small caliber pistols and practice with them. Then I suggest we form a Karate and Judo Club. With such clubs—and let's face it, there are scores of clubs for athletic and other reasons already existing in Lagrangia—no one will look twice. We'll be able to take outings in the wilderness areas where we can drill and study the works of such old time guerrillas as Che Guevara and Mao. We'll put ourselves in condition to face the crisis when it comes."

Somebody else called, "What else, Balt?"

He said, "We're going to have to infiltrate this Sons of Liberty organization, not only here in Grissom but in all of the Islands. We have to keep track of what they're up to. Undoubtedly, it's a strictly adult outfit so only the oldest among us would stand a chance of joining them. I suggest here in Grissom that Jim, Tom and I seek them out and join up."

He looked over at the chairman of the meeting. "That okay with you, Jim?"

The other bobbed his Adam's apple. "Count me in."

Tom M-I/3-O-08-ST6571 called up from the audience, "Wizard, Balt. I always wanted to be a spy."

Somebody laughed and said to the slightly plumpish teenager, "When they catch you, Tom, you're allowed to name your last breakfast."

"That's why I've always wanted to be a spy," he called back.

After the meeting had terminated, after several committees had been named, including two to look into the matter of forming a Young People's Hunting Club and a Karate and Judo Club, Balt, Jim, Tom and Martha left the hall together.

Tom said, "This cloak and dagger stuff is wizard but how do we locate the outfit so that we can infiltrate them?"

He was an overweight boy in the same age group as Balt, with the bright eyes that were seemingly a built-in characteristic of all these youngsters. The members of the 150 Club not only had far above average intelligence, they projected it.

Balt said, "According to Martha, her father and possibly her mother belong to it. I'll go home with her this evening and see if I can get a lead. If I can get in, then I'll swing something so that you two can, also."

Martha said, "Wait a minute. You're not going to do anything that will get Dad in trouble, are you?"

Balt looked at her. "Probably not. Probably *I'm* the one who'll get in trouble. These Elitists, or Sons of Liberty, whatever we call them, are not playing games. And sooner or later it's either us or them. You're a member of the 150 Club, Martha. Are you with us or not?"

"Oh, I'm with you, I suppose."

"Then let's go back to your house."

She cocked her head at him. "To resume what we were doing before the meeting?"

He snorted at that and said, "Knock, knock."

She took him in suspiciously. "Who's there?"

"Chesterfield."

"Chesterfield who?"

"Chesterfield your arms around me, darling."

"I wonder," she muttered, "if there's a lobotomy that would cut out the bum jokes, and leave the rest of you."

Chapter Ten

Rex, Susie, King and Virginia Dare were having a council of war when Balt entered. They hadn't got very far. They had discussed the shooting out in the wilderness but nobody could come up with even a guess at who had been guilty of the attempt.

Rex had said, "I assume that I've made some enemies in my years here in Island Three, but I can't think of any who would want to shoot me."

King said, "The timing rules out anything from the past. It has to have been somebody connected with this Elitist thing."

"Probably," Susie said.

"I wish to hell I'd been able to wing him," Rex growled. "But he was too far off for my pistol."

Balt came in and slumped into a chair. "What spins?" he said.

"Not much, son," the retired detective told him. "King's pointed out that both the delegation from Elysium and Theodor Karadja are staying at his hotel, the Lagrange Hilton, which isn't surprising since that's where practically all non-Lagrangists reside when in Grissom. We've been trying to figure out some method by which King could get a line on them. Unfortunately, he isn't exactly a trained second-story man. And, frankly, I'm too old to be sneaking around on balconies, or whatever."

Virginia Dare said to Balt, "Where have you been, dear?"

"Getting a line on these local Elitists."

All eyes took him in.

"And?" Susie said. "Don't be so gloatingly superior."

Balt said, "They don't call themselves Elitists here in Grissom except maybe among themselves. They call themselves the Sons of Liberty. Well, there's a sister organization for women, The Daughters of Liberty."

"Sons of Liberty!" Both Rex and Susie got out.

King looked at them and said, "You know about the outfit?"

"We know about them, all right," Rex told him. "But I had no idea that they were still in existence." He looked at Susie. "Maybe it's a revival."

Virginia Dare said, "I don't believe I've ever heard of such an organization in Lagrange Five."

"You were too young," Susie told her. "Only a child." She looked back at King. "It was in the early days, before we declared our independence from the Reunited Nations. The Sons of Liberty was a Lagrangist organization that was divided into two more or less equal groups. One group, to which the Professor and I belonged, was called the Conservatives. We wanted eventual independence but we were in favor of taking it easy, until the Satellite Solar Power Stations were in full swing, beaming microwave energy down to Earth. Then we'd be self-sufficient and no longer dependent on appropriations from the Reunited Nations. But the other group we called the Radicals; they not only wanted to sever connections immediately but insisted we make some basic changes in the Lagrangist socioeconomic system which was already evolving at the time."

"What changes?" King said. "I thought you had roughly the same system we have in the Promised Land Islands. In fact, I thought we'd copied it from you."

"That's right," the old man said. "The early Lagrangists developed a system that amounted to an up-graded type of nineteenth century syndicalism. All types of work were divided into categories, or functions as they're usually called; Manufacturing, Communications, Transportation, Medicine, Education, Entertainment, Agriculture, Statistics, and so on. Within each function the different groups of workers would elect their foremen. The foremen in turn would get together and elect the supervisors of each sub-department. Then the supervisors would get together and from their number elect a Councilor to represent their function on the Council, which was a planning body rather than anything else. Since absolute abundance was produced for everybody, no system of exchange was used. It was the old slogan, from each according to his abilities, to each according to his needs. Not

even members of the Council received any more
than anyone else. They didn't have to."

"Well, that's about how we handle it," King said.
"Maybe some minor differences. But what did this
radical group of your Sons of Liberty want to do?"

"Turn it upside down," the other told him.
"They claimed that democracy was inefficient; that
it had never worked anywhere. That the less competent, by definition, were incompetent to elect
their superiors. So they wanted the Councilors in
each function to appoint the supervisors below
them and for the supervisors to appoint the fore-
man below them. It was something like the Tech-
nocracy, Inc. plan of the 1930s. At the very top
there'd be a High Councilor, or whatever they
wanted to call him."

"I don't see what would be accomplished,"
Virginia Dare said.

Balt was listening intently. He said, "What
would this High Councilor and the Council get out
of it?"

Susie said contemptuously, "They'd be sitting in
the catbird seat. They wanted to revive such institutions as servants for the benefit of Councilors and
supervisors and, among other privileges, limou-
sines for those in power. Bicycles were beneath
them."

"In short," King said, "these so-called Radicals,
among the Sons of Liberty, were to be an elite."

"That's right," Rex said. "There were some
other angles, too. They wanted to go down to Earth
and set the earthworms right. Get it? To take over,
end the periodic wars, enforce rules on pollution,

manage the utilization of raw materials and other resources, clean up the oceans, overthrow corrupt governments. That sort of thing."

"Well," Balt said. "That part of it doesn't sound so bad. Earth can use some cleaning up."

Susie looked over at him and said, "Reforms come from within a people, they aren't imposed from outside, or from above, Balt. When a people are ready for changes, they make them. There is no such thing as a benevolent dictatorship because it's up to the dictators to decide what's benevolent. Your classic example is the Soviet Complex. Since 1917, the Party has been giving the people what it decided was good for them. Evidently, the man in the street didn't think so."

Virginia Dare said, "Where did you learn about this, Balt?"

"A girl friend—you know Martha—told me. Her father belongs to it. Her mother too, I guess."

Susie said slowly, "It makes sense. Largely, the Sons of Liberty broke up after we declared our independence. The reason for its existence had been achieved, so there was no reason for its continuing. But if the Elitists are recruiting here in Lagrangia, using the name Sons of Liberty would give them excellent cover. There are tens of thousands of Lagrangists who used to belong twenty-five years ago. They'd have no objection to listening to the new message; no prejudices against their fellow former members."

"I think you're right," the retired detective said. "At least we ought to dig into it a little. Check them out."

"One difficulty there," Susie said, "is that you and I both fought the Radical wing of the Sons of Liberty. In fact, we were highly responsible for their coming a cropper. If they're back in action, they'll be watching us."

Something came to Rex and he said, sourly, "Or even shooting at us."

King looked over at him. "You think?"

"It makes as much sense as anything else."

Virginia Dare said, "Why don't we check up on them in the data banks? No matter how secretive they try to be, there should be something there."

"Not from this apartment," Rex said. "If they're keeping an eye on us, they might have us monitored someway or other. Most likely, they even have representatives in Communications and working in the data banks. In the early days of Lagrange Five, electronic bugs weren't here. But who knows now? The information on how to make them is all in the data banks. Maybe our Elitist friends have them. I've already checked out this apartment and couldn't locate any, but they might be able to tap our TV phone calls."

Virginia Dare nodded and said, even while coming to her feet, "Suppose that King and I go to my place and work from there? We'll try and discover if there're any records of them."

King said, standing too, "Wizard. Sounds like a good idea. We have no other leads."

Virginia Dare said, "Balt? Coming?"

He said, "I've got a date tonight."

Virginia Dare and King left, went down to the street and secured the inevitable bikes.

She said, "I live out a way, about three miles into the mountains. I don't really like cities as big as New Frisco."

"Wizard," he said. "Let's go." He flung a leg over his bicycle and pushed off.

As they pedalled along he said, "I'll have to find the opportunity to see more of Grissom. We haven't anything larger than an Island Two in the asteroid belt. This dwarfs our places."

"You should see Island Four," Virginia Dare told him. "It dwarfs Grissom."

He looked ahead appreciatively at the mountain scenery. He said, "I'd settle for this. I think our engineers, working on our Island Three, should come and take a look at Grissom. They'd get some good ideas and be able to avoid whatever mistakes you might have made."

She said, slowly, "Island Five was scheduled to be *really* something. Seventy-five miles long and it could have housed over so many millions of people, each with something like five acres of land at his disposal."

"Seventy-five miles?" He shook his head. "I suppose that theoretically there's no limit, so long as there are asteroids to mine. But it'd sure as hell take a long time to build, automation or not."

They had left the outskirts of New Frisco and were now pedalling up into the foothills. As he had noticed before, the climb was not exhausting, since gravity lessened as they ascended.

She blurted out of a clear sky, "What in the name of Zen motivates them, King?" Then, when she realized that he didn't understand, "The Elitists: why do they want to take over?"

He thought about it, before saying, "I suppose the power urge we have always had with us. It's not material gain they want. Here in Lagrangia and out in my asteroid belt, we have affluence beyond the dreams of avarice of the older generations down Earthside. But the power urge is another thing. Take Alexander the Great: he had all Greece at his feet. What motivated him to cross to Asia Minor, overwhelm Persia and then continue on to India? Or Ghengis Khan or Tamerlane? Or, in Mexico, what motivated Pancho Villa? Yes, Madero and Zapata were idealists, fighting for a cause. But not Villa; he had no ideals. What motivated either Hitler or Stalin? Certainly, we recognize that Goering and Goebbels were opportunists, out to feather their own nests. But what motivated Hitler? The desire for power over his fellow man. I think that the classic example was when somebody asked John Kennedy why he wanted to be President. Supposedly, he already had everything; wealth, a beautiful wife, security. To the question, he answered, 'Because that's where the power is.' "

She shivered in feminine rejection and said, "I still don't understand it."

King said, "Actually, neither do I. But look at this beautiful little town up ahead. If the travel Tri-Di shows I've seen are correct, this looks like a small mountain village in Switzerland."

She smiled, "It's Heidi. This is where I live. Almost all towns in Grissom are built with a motif. We have Italian hill towns. We have Elizabethan

era English villages, complete with thatched roofs.
There are several Germanic towns of different peri-
ods, not to speak of Oriental ones. Usually, the resi-
dents even go to the extreme of wearing authentic
costumes. You know, *lederhosen* and so forth here in
Heidi."

"It's a darn good idea," King admitted as they
pedalled into the single main street of the Alpine
village. She had been right; most of the pedestrians,
strolling along, wore Swiss costumes of a century
or more ago. Some of the men even had long, intri-
cately decorated, curved pipes, probably of cherry
wood.

There was an antique looking *gasthaus* from
which accordian and zither music was issuing forth
and the singing of drinking songs.

Virginia Dare laughed. "We even have a group
that practices yodeling. It's awful."

They headed up a narrow side-street and out a bit
from the center of Heidi.

"This is my house," she said, coming to a halt
before a small chalet that looked like an illustration
in a children's book.

"Why, it's charming," he told her. "You people
have gone far beyond us in these things. Up in the
belt, we're more frenetic, not so colorful. Not so
artistic, I suppose I should say."

The interior kept up the motif. It was almost like
a doll house. The furniture looked antique but, of
course, couldn't have been. It was wood, though,
which somewhat surprised King.

She said, "Wooden furniture is still on the scarce
side. But they spoil me. As the first child born in

space, people go out of their way, as Uncle Rex and Aunt Susie did when I was orphaned. How about a drink, King? Keeping up with the Swiss atmosphere, I have some excellent black cherry brandy, or Kirsch, if you'd prefer."

"I'll take the brandy," he said, lowering himself into a rocking chair which had embroidered doilies on its arms.

She went over to a handcarved sideboard which held several bottles and glasses, poured two small glasses of a dark red liquid, and returned with them.

Both sipped and King congratulated her on the delicious liqueur.

Virginia Dare said, "I suppose that we should get the show on the road." She put her glass down and went over to the small ornate desk that sat under a curtained window.

She sat before the TV phone screen, the only modern looking device in the room, save for the lights, and dialed. She said something into the screen; dialed again. From where he sat, King Ford couldn't hear the conversation.

By the time she returned, he had finished his cherry brandy and she absently refilled his glass and took up her own, before taking a chair across from him. She was frowning.

"What did you come up with?" he said.

"Nothing. And *that* is unlikely enough to give me goosebumps. No leads we can follow up. There's nothing in the data banks about the Sons of Liberty following the declaration of independence from the Reunited Nations and Earth. But Balt was so definite. And from what Rex and Susie said, it certainly sounded like a Lagrangia version of the Elysium Elitists."

"That's what I thought."

She said, "There's only one explanation. They've infiltrated the Communications Function to the point where they can tamper with the data being fed into the banks. If so, we have really got a problem."

"In more ways than one," he nodded. "There's nothing more important to a revolutionary group than to get control of the communications system. If they can take over from the inside, they've got it made."

They sat in dejection for a time.

Finally, he said, "Well, we've achieved exactly nothing. I suppose I should go on back to Rex and Susie and report." He looked about the room and said, "You know, this is possibly the most charming living room that I've ever seen. Do you and Balt live here alone?"

She made a rueful mouth. "Balt lives here *sometimes*. He's gotten to the age where I don't know where he is, or what he's doing most of the time. I suppose that he's just beginning to get into the full swing of sex."

"Where's his father?"

She smiled, ruefully again. "I haven't the vaguest idea. Not only where, but who."

He looked at her.

She said, "King, we've left most of the old sexual institutions behind, here in Lagrangia. The original reasons for most of them are anachronistic. I don't believe my own father and mother were married, and that was over 35 years ago. I don't know who Balt's father was. I was going with several men at the time, back when I was seventeen or eighteen."

He said uncomfortably, "In the Promised Land Islands we keep track for genetic and statistical reasons. We're more or less phasing out marriage as such but we try to keep track of who a child's father was, for medical reasons. Obviously it's easier to keep track of who the mother was."

She said, "Yes, the old saying, it's a wise child that knows its father."

"But if you don't keep track, how do you prevent, well, just short of incestuous relations, with their results?"

Virginia Dare said, "You know, common belief to the contrary, such relationships aren't necessarily regressive. For instance, Cleopatra, who was certainly a very intelligent and capable woman, as well as being beautiful, was the result of a long line of brother and sister marriages, and when the Romans first came, she herself was married to her own brother. All the Ptolemies did it, for the purpose of keeping the throne of the Pharaohs in the family. And certainly you know about line breeding in animals." Then she added, "But ordinarily in Lagrangia before a couple expose themselves to parenthood they look into their bloodlines and check how close of kin they might be."

He stood, preparatory to leaving, and said, "Well, I still say it's a beautiful house."

"Let me show you the rest of it."

She led him from room to room.

They wound up in her bedroom, an utterly feminine chamber in full keeping with her fragile beauty.

And suddenly, without either of them knowing how, they were in each other's arms. Her full breasts were against his chest, the nipples hardening as he pressed her half-open mouth with his own.

How long it was before they stepped apart, neither knew. His dark eyes were smoldering, hers were sloe.

She said, "But this is impossible, King. Why, I'm old enough to be your . . ."

He said hoarsely, "My older sister, nothing more. What difference do a few years make?"

She looked down at him, still breathing deeply and said, "Well, I can see that I can't let you go home like that."

"What?" he said blankly.

She went over to the bed and pulled the cover down, then turned back to him and said slyly, "I can tell you love me by the expression on your pants."

Chapter Eleven

As they rode back toward her house, Martha looked over at Balt and said, "Those knock-knock jokes of yours are strictly from maize."

He pretended indignation. "You're not intellectual enough to understand them."

"Ha," she said. "There was a better line of yaks from an even earlier period. You simply take an old saying, or a quote and drop one word off the end of it."

He glanced over at her. "What's funny about that?"

"Well, for instance, *It's an ill wind that blows nobody*."

He snorted, "Holy Jumping Zen, it'd take you to come up with one like that."

She said, "How about, *You can lead a horse to water but you can't make her*."

Balt said, "Wizard, but that's a take-off on a knock-knock. Knock, knock."

She sighed in resignation. "Who's there?"

"Horticulture."

"Horticulture who?"

"You can lead a horticulture but you can't make her think."

"I've had it," she told him. "Listen, what's our approach to Dad?"

"I don't know. We'll just have to play it by ear. You're sure he belongs to this Sons of Liberty outfit?"

"He's avid," she told him definitely. "He has nothing else to do, for that matter. He hasn't worked for over two years. He was trained as an agronomist and agriculture has been automated to the point that I doubt if more than a couple of hundred are employed in Grissom and Komarov combined. And, of course, since they've cancelled the building of Island Five there's nothing in the line of setting up new systems."

He looked over at her, from the side of his eyes and said, "Look, what would the old boy say if he knew that you were laying for me?"

She was surprised at the question. "Why should he care? I've been getting poked since I was fourteen." She thought about it. "No, thirteen. And I liked it the first time I did it and every time since."

They pulled up before her home, racked their wheels and went on in.

Fredric M-I/2-A-90 HHl783 was seated before the Tri-Di screen, looking pleased at whatever he was seeing and hearing. He looked up at their entrance.

He was a man in his mid-thirties, square of face, unhappy of expression usually though not now, and looked something like Rudolph Hess at the time of the Nazi take-over. He was nervous of mannerism and had little humor in his make-up. He seemed an unlikely parent for Martha.

He said, "Hello, Balt. What spins?"

Balt said, "Not much." He slumped into a chair, teenage fashion, and said, "What's on the air?"

"Damn good speech by Lonzo, Councilor for the Education Function. We need more men like him."

Martha had gone on into her bedroom.

The younger man said, "Oh? What was he talking about? I've heard some speeches by Lonzo before. Usually makes a lot of sense."

Fredric looked at him in approval. "I didn't know you young people had any interest in Lagrangian affairs."

"Oh, sure. You'd be surprised. A lot of us don't think much of the way things are going these days."

Fredric nodded. "That's just what Lonzo was getting at. He claims that the present system is going to pot and that what we're going to have to do is reexamine our basic institutions and change them to get us out of the rut."

"Holy Zen," Balt said. "And I thought I was the only one with ideas like that. Possibly the old ways applied back when Lagrange Five was first being pioneered but things have changed." He chewed an offending cuticle innocently.

The older man was obviously taken aback. In common with too many adults, he didn't expect much from the young. He launched into his favorite theme.

"It's like Lonzo was saying on the Tri-Di. Those who originally planned the Lagrange Five Project should have consulted the anthropologists further. Professor Casey and the others seemed to naively believe that the Islands would duplicate the culture of Earth. But the environment is different, the way of life is different, the socioeconomic setup is different, but especially the people are different. Given the emigration requirements that skim the cream from Earth, we spacers are not going to ape the earthworms. Why should a superior people copy an inferior one's institutions?"

"Right," Balt chimed in enthusiastically, though the other had said nothing new to him. In fact, Martha's father sounded like somewhat of a cloddy.

Fredric pressed on. "Much of a culture is dependent upon environmental factors and the form of making a living. For instance, take a tribe Earthside in primitive times, dependent upon agriculture and living in an arid area. When it turns to religion, invariably it develops a rain god. The same doesn't apply in an area which has a more than adequate rainfall. Or take a tribe of nomads, dependent upon the chase. They'll invariably have gods to call upon to provide an abundance of game."

His earnest young listener was nodding. "Marx's Materialist Conception of History," he said.

The other frowned. "What?"

"Nothing. Something I was reading the other day."

"At any rate," Fredric said, "instead of our copying their institutions, they should be copying ours. We should take up our responsibilities and lead them."

Balt took a chance: "After we force a few changes up here," he hinted.

Fredric was impressed. He came to his feet, saying, "Like a drink, Balt? I suppose you're old enough to be drinking."

"Oh, sure. I'm older than I look. But no thanks. I prefer trank."

His host went over to the bar set in one corner and began making himself a pseudo-whiskey and water. He said, "You can get hooked on that, can't you?"

"Trank? I suppose so, if you take enough of it long enough. But it's no problem. The Medical Function can cure addiction in a matter of hours. But there's a hooker in the cure. From then on in, for the rest of your life, you can't stand the sight of the stuff. You'll never take trank again."

Martha's father came back with his drink and reseated himself. "Where were we?" he said.

But Balt changed the subject by saying, "Martha was telling me about that picnic you took her to. A group of elitists, she said, whatever that means."

The other looked a bit unhappy. "We avoid that term," he told the young visitor. "We call ourselves the Sons of Liberty. But, in actuality, that's what it amounts to. The elite of Lagrangia should take over."

"That's what I say," the teenager told him. "Too many people just sit around doing nothing. They don't have any gumption. Just because you have an I.Q. of over 130 doesn't mean you're going to use it. Even among the most intelligent there are the leaders and the led. And the leaders *should* lead, and the others follow."

Fredric, now with real respect mirrored in his face, said, "I couldn't have put it better myself. You say Martha told you about the Sons of Liberty? I didn't realize she was really interested."

"Oh, Martha isn't as scatterbrained as she pretends. How old do you have to be to join the Sons of Liberty?"

The older man scowled and thought about it. "Why, I don't know, Balt. So far as I know, it's never come up."

The boy's expression indicated that a sudden inspired thought had come to him. "You know," he said. "Martha mentioned that you had a sort of women's auxiliary organization, the Daughters of Liberty. Why shouldn't there be a young people's auxiliary that we could join until we were old enough to become full members? You know, something like the *Komsomols*, the Young Communists in the Soviet Complex, or the Boy Scouts. People who are too young to be in the National Guard, or the Army or Navy, but like to wear uniforms, march, salute and all."

"Why, it sounds like a good idea to me," Fredric said. "We're just about to launch an all out recruiting campaign; to really begin to spread the message. I'll bring it up at the next Central Commitee meeting. I'm a member. I've got an idea that Bert would go for a youth auxiliary."

"What's a good idea?" Martha said, reentering the living room.

Balt was enthusiastic. "Your father's going to

recommend that there be a youth auxiliary of the Sons of Liberty. Are you in, Martha?"

She looked at him wryly. "You've come a long way in a short time," she said. "But I suppose so."

Balt said to Fredric, "I've got two friends, Jim and Tom, I've been talking to along the same line. They'll come in."

The older man, obviously pleased, finished his drink and got up to refresh it.

"You kids'll have a great time," he said. "Something to do. Parades, public rallies and all. We've designed a sort of uniform we're all going to wear. A men's version and a women's. There's no reason why we can't have a young people's version too."

"Sounds wizard," Balt said. "Who's this Bert you mentioned?"

"The top man. He's the Councilor for Transportation, on the Grissom Council. When we've put over our program, he's going to be the New High Councilor. He's the most competent man in Island Three."

Balt refrained from asking him how that conclusion had been reached.

But he didn't have to. Fredric said, "The way we figure is that in any society the best men get to the top. It's been that way all through history. Napoleon became Emperor of France because he was the best man, the same as Caesar in Rome."

"Of course," Balt agreed readily. "And if something happens so that a next-best character takes the lead because he's inherited the position, or something, then the more competent below overthrow him and take over."

However, Balt recalled what Rex and Susie had said about benevolent dictatorships and also what he himself had said in his speech to the Young People's 150 Club, about the rule of a self-proclaimed elite. Once a clique gets into power, it calls itself an elite whether it is or not. He reminded himself that the 150 Club was a true elite, not merely a self-proclaimed one. This Bert, the head of the Sons of Liberty, must have a lot of credibility if he had been elected Councilor of the Transportation Function, but that didn't mean he was the best suited to be High Councilor if and when that position was established.

He said, "Sir, what's the program? How do we expect to come to power so that we can make all these changes that the Sons of Liberty want?"

"That's a good question," Martha murmured.

Fredric was all caught up in the explanation of his favorite subject. He took back another slug of his drink and said, "When we're ready, we're going to call for a referendum. Now, what you've got to remember is that precious few people get really interested in these matters. Most remain lethargic. A comparatively small but well organized group can often put over a political or socioeconomic change. Take the Bolsheviks, in Russia. There were only a few thousand of them and only a dozen or so were real leaders; Lenin, Trotsky, Rykov, Bukharin, Zinoviev, Radek. But they were tight-knit and knew what they wanted in a time of confusion. Or take the American Revolution. People like Paine, Sam Adams, Jefferson, Madison, knew what they wanted. As far as the people were concerned, possibly ten percent were avid patriots and ten percent Tories. The other eighty percent just didn't give a damn. If the British were in control of an area, they supported the British. If Washington's army was around, they supported the revolutionists."

"What's that got to do with Lagrangia?" Martha said. In spite of what Balt had said to her earlier in regard to her I.Q., she was obviously sharper than her father. As a Lagrangist, he had to have one of at least 130, but, as a third generation Lagrangist, hers was above 150. Little nymphomaniac Martha was a genius.

Her parent looked at her impatiently. "We're organized. The opposition isn't. Jean . . ." he looked over at Balt ". . . who represents Statistics in the Council—we have several Sons of Liberty in the Council—reported on a recent opposition session. They're completely at sea. No program at all for ending such problems as unemployment, the drop in the birthrate, the falling off of emigration, the grinding to a halt of building new Islands. They'll be putty in our hands."

Balt said, "Then you think . . ."

Fredric said definitely, "We have a program; they don't. Any program is better than none at all. The Lagrangists will listen to us. Out of pure ennui, if nothing else, they'll vote for us. Some will do it thinking, *'give them a chance and see what happens; anything is better than what we've got now.'* "

Balt nodded. He said, "Wizard, but I suggest that you point out to Bert that a nucleus of an opposition to the Sons of Liberty is beginning to form. Rex Bader, Doctor Susie Hawkins, as she used to be called, and a newcomer from the asteroid belt, King Ford, are becoming active. My mother, Virginia Dare, is associated with them. All three carry considerable weight in Lagrangia. If the elite is ever to come to power, they will have to be dealt with."

Later, when Balt and Martha were alone, she looked at him and said, "Why, you traitorous bastard. Even your own mother . . ."

"We're not playing games," he said coldly. "Besides, they would have found out very shortly anyway. Rex, Susie, King and my mother aren't hiding anything. As it is, I'm in. Otherwise, when it came up that I was the son of Virginia Dare and she was in the enemy camp, they would have been leery of me."

Chapter Twelve

Frol Pogodin, alias Phil M-E-A-98-PT-2376, pedalled up to the Grissom Administration Building in New Frisco. He wore a pair of overalls upon the back of which was stitched in heavy yellow thread MAINTENANCE. He parked his bike and took from its rear luggage rack a fairly large tool kit.

Whistling absently, tool kit in hand, he strode toward the entry, noticed by nobody. He went on through the lobby, still noticed by nobody.

Frol Pogodin was a man in his late twenties who by no means looked like an espionage-counterespionage operative. He would have been taken as an American of the usual mixed ancestry, Northern European or the British Isles predominating. He had pleasant, easy-going features and a somewhat shy expression. Frol Pogodin had never once been suspected in his five years of service to the Party.

He went up the stairs, whistling, to the sixth floor. He stode down the corridor to the Conference

Room of the Council, nonchalantly opened up the door and stepped in.

The sole occupant of the room was Paul, Councilor of Agriculture. He sat at the end of the heavy long table, staring glumly at a sheaf of papers before him. He looked up at the other's entrance.

"Maintenance," Pogodin said.

"Oh?" Paul said. "What's wrong?"

"Damned if I know. Computers threw a few lights on this room. Probably nothing much." The supposed repairman put his tool kit on the table and opened it.

Paul turned back to his papers.

Frol Pogodin brought forth an instrument with a pistol grip, flicked a stud which set it to a disturbing buzzing and began to go about the room, pointing it at anything pertaining to electronics.

Paul put down his stylo, scowled and said, "How long are you going to be making bug music with that thing?"

"Darned if I know," Pogodin said. "Should take me only a few minutes to find. Then I'll have to repair it. If I'm bothering you, maybe I could come back later. I've got a couple of other stops I have to make."

Paul sighed, came to his feet and gathered up the papers. "Never mind," he said. "I can go to my office." Without looking at the alleged maintenance man again, he left the Conference Room, closing the door behind him. Five minutes later, he couldn't have described the agent.

Pogodin flicked off his buzzing device and put it back into the tool kit and brought forth a small gizmo which looked like a black button. He got down on his hands and knees and crawled under the desk. At one corner, right up against one of the heavy legs, the button stuck firmly. He moved back a little and stared at it contemplatively. It was very inconspicuous, and, even if seen, might have been taken for part of the table.

He moved forward again and tapped his fingernail on the table leg. He said, in Russian, "Testing, testing."

The voice of Theodor Karadja came back, very thin but quite audible. It said, "Receiving, receiving."

Pogodin crawled out from under the table again and went to the far end of the room, turned in the direction of the wireless electronic bug and said, again, "Testing, testing." He went from one area of the room to the others and each time repeated the same words.

Then he went back under the table and said, "Receiving?"

"Yes, clearly," the other's voice came through. "Now get over to Bert's house and plant one there. Comrade Shvets reports that he isn't home. He's probably already on his way here. He lives alone, so you shouldn't have much difficulty."

"Yes, Comrade Major," Pogodin said.

He crawled back from under the table and snapped shut the tool kit. Whistling softly again, he left the conference hall and went down the steps, still once again noticed by no one.

It was approximately an hour later that Bert, Jean and Field Marshal Van Eckmann entered the hall. They took chairs, Bert sitting in the chairman's position at the end of the table, the others flanking him.

The Sons of Liberty head looked at his watch and said, "He's not due for another half hour."

"Wizard," Jean said. "It'll give us a chance to discuss what we think about his offers."

Van Eckmann looked at her and said, "You don't trust him?"

Jean, Councilor of the Statistics Function, was a painfully plain woman in her early thirties. Just by looking into her customarily drawn face, one could see the brilliance behind it. Inwardly bitter, she made no effort to gild what little nature had given her. Her hair was drawn back tightly into an anachronistic bun; her lips and eyes were totally innocent of cosmetics and gave the impression that they had always been so.

"Would anyone trust an agent of the Soviet Complex?" she said scornfully. "Since the days of Lenin they have followed the Machiavellian precept, the ends justify the means. And what have the ends always been? The world revolution. The domination of the Party over all."

"He admitted that," Bert said, grudgingly. "Evidently, the Party thinks that at long last the cold war is coming to an end, with them winning. For some reason or other, they need Lagrangia in order to bring about this economic collapse which will lead all present nations to join the Soviet Complex."

"Yes," she said. "And then what is to prevent them from taking us over in return?"

Van Eckmann said, "He claims that all they want is the ability to take over command of their former nationals, here in Lagrange Five, the scientists and so forth."

"That's what he *claims*," Jean said flatly.

"What is the alternative to coming in with him?" Bert said. "If we don't, he threatened Elysium."

"I wouldn't worry too much about that," the self-named Field Marshal said confidently. "I didn't say anything at the time, but we aren't as defenseless as all that. As a matter of fact, we are already at work producing atomic weapons. The asteroid belt is a year out from Earth. The moment we detected one of their space cruisers, or even an automated spacecraft carrying a bomb coming in our direction, we would get a fix on it and deploy our counterattack. They'd never get close enough to utilize their so-called laser rifles and other weapons."

"Ummm," Bert said. "Admittedly, our technology is at least as good as theirs, especially in any field pertaining to space, though admittedly they have greater resources." He looked at Jean and repeated his question. "What are the alternatives?"

"Our original plan could still stand. That is, the anarchists in Elysium have been overthrown and the Elitists have taken over. The next step is for the Sons of Liberty to take over here in Lagrangia. Elysium is then in a position to assume control of the Asteroid Federation, without fear of interference. The next goal, then, is Earth itself."

Bert said, "Yes. That was originally so, but our

weapon was the threat to discontinue microwaving solar power to Earthside industry, but this Pierre Cannes tells us that the Soviet Complex is not really dependent on that source of power. We could collapse the economies of the West, but not that of the Soviet Complex."

Jean nodded. "Yes, that is what he said but there is another aspect. The fact that Soviet nationals almost to a man have defected the moment they come to Lagrangia is an indication of the feelings of the Soviet peoples. They too look up to us. They too would probably prefer to be led by us in space, rather than their present Soviet bureaucracy which has never, in the past century, been anything but inefficient."

Bert and the Elitist from Elysium looked at her thoughtfully.

Jean said, "He seems to think that he can be of aid to us, at this stage. Wizard; let's go along with him. Perhaps he can. But then, once we are in power, we shall see what we shall see. The teachings of Machiavelli can be utilized by anyone, not just the Party."

The Field Marshal grunted in an attempt at humor. "Dirty pool," he said.

Bert and Jean laughed, and Bert said, "If you sit down to a poker game in which everyone else is cheating, you're a dizzard if you don't too. And I suspect that Jean is right. This Pierre Cannes is double dealing, one way or the other."

The plain-faced woman nodded. "As I see it, we go through our plans here. Once in control in Lagrangia we give Elysium the go-ahead and they take over the Asteroid Federation. We then contact Earth and give them our ultimatum, threatening to discontinue our beaming of solar power. That will force the West to submit. Once the West is in our control, we will start beaming messages to the Soviet Complex urging the people to join with all the rest of humanity, into one great federation—under our control, of course. By this time they should be glad of an excuse to dump the Party."

"I suppose that's about it," Bert said.

"Yes," the Field Marshal said.

There came a knock at the door and their eyes went to it.

"That must be him," Bert muttered. "Right on time."

Theodor Karadja entered, his dark eyes bright, his ever-ready smile on his lips. "Good afternoon, Comrades," he said.

Bert and Van Eckmann got up to shake hands.

The espionage troubleshooter took a chair only two down from the rest of them. "I hope that I didn't interrupt anything," he said.

"Certainly not," Bert told him hurriedly. "We were just discussing our mutual plans."

Jean said, "As a matter of fact, we were wondering in just what manner you could be of assistance to us. You mentioned that when you first entered into our . . . conference."

"Yes, of course." The Rumanian looked at her. "I suspect that you people are inexperienced in the ways of conspiracy and of revolution. We of the Soviet Complex, to the contrary, are possibly the most experienced revolutionaries of all times. We

have put them over in a score of countries from
China to Cuba. Through me, you will be able to
draw on that experience."

Bert said, "For instance, what would your advice
be immediately? We're new to this. Abilities we
might have, but practical background, no."

The other made a gesture of acceptance. "For one
thing, I suggest that you move as rapidly as possible. As matters stand now, you have an organization with a definite program. The opposition, to the
extent that there is one at all, is not organized. You
must not give them the time to become so. Strike
fast, and strike ruthlessly."

"What do you mean by ruthlessly?" Jean said.

He smiled over at her, a predator's smile. "Just
that, Comrade. As your movement begins to take
effect, elements are going to oppose you. Hit them
hard."

Bert ran a hand through his sandy hair and said,
"I'm not sure just how the average Lagrangists
would accept violence, if we're to take your advice
literally."

"They need not know the source of the blows,"
the other told him. "Your basic premise, which you
present to your people, is that Lagrangia has
become inefficient; that the present elected Council
is incapable of directing your socioeconomic system. It is simply not effective and matters are
deteriorating. Very well, if in the midst of your
flinging these accusations some of the most influential Lagrangists were, ah, injured, seemingly by
malcontents, it would be one more proof that the

Council was inept and the people would be more receptive to the idea of a strong hand at the helm."

Jean said, unhappily, "I'm afraid that the Sons of Liberty, in common with other Lagrangists, are scientists, technicians, engineers, highly trained and competent experts in every function. But we are not strongarm people. I can't think of any of us who either could, or would, attack even our enemies."

"Ah," he flashed his smile again. "But I and my men are, ah, strongarm people, as you put it. We have been known to eliminate our enemies on various occasions."

They stared at him.

He said slowly, "At this stage, are there any persons that you already fear? That is, any who should be liquidated before they can become heads of an opposition?"

The three looked at each other.

Marshal Van Eckmann said deliberately, "When my colleagues and I came here to act as a liaison group with our fellows in Lagrangia, the Asteroid Federation sent a young man after us. His name is King Ford and he has prestige through his father, Whip Ford. Whip holds somewhat the same position in the asteroid belt as did the late Professor George Casey in Lagrange Five. That is, he is often called the Father of the Promised Land. We were warned about King's arrival and kept check on him. He immediately made contact with Susie, formerly Doctor Susie Hawkins, who was Professor Casey's secretary, and with a former detective, Rex Bader, who was once the professor's bodyguard."

Karadja's eyes flickered at the word, 'bodyguard'. He turned to Bert. "Tell me more about this Susie Hawkins and Rex Bader."

Bert said, "They're both old timers, among the original space pioneers. Before Lagrangia declared its independence, they were among the most active of the opponents of our wing of the first Sons of Liberty. In fact, largely through their efforts, we were all but destroyed. Following independence, the Sons of Liberty became dormant; in fact, the Conservative wing, which they supported, disappeared. Our wing continued, but barely. Only recently have we revived."

The Soviet hatchetman said, "I see. Then we can suspect that this Rex Bader and Susie Hawkins, in conjunction with King Ford, can be expected to attempt to frustrate our plans."

Jean said, "Both of the first two are on the elderly side. I doubt if they could do much."

Karadja smiled at her and said, "My dear Comrade Jean, Karl Marx was an old man when he wrote *Das Kapital*, possibly the most influential revolutionary book of all time. And Lenin was by no means a young man when he led the Bolsheviks to victory." His eyes went back to Bert. "This Rex Bader; a detective and a former bodyguard? I take it he would not scare easily."

"I would judge that he is the only man on Grissom—aside from you—experienced in violence."

Jean said, and there was an unwonted unhappiness in her voice, "See here! Susie is possibly the most popular person in Lagrangia. She has even been made an honorary member of the Council, though she heads no function. If anything happened to her . . .''

The Rumanian's eyebrows went up. "If anything happened to her, the Lagrangists would become indignant that the government had deteriorated to such a point that popular citizens were not protected."

Before Jean could reply, he said to Bert, "I suggest that in your program you demand that a police force be formed to enforce safety. You'll be wanting such a force in the future, at any rate. In fact, within your Sons of Liberty organization you might begin such a police embryo. Strong young men who can attend each of your rallies and public meetings. I particularly recommend those who seem to have a grudge against the facts of life; surely you can find a few sturdy neurotics. They can be equipped with short clubs and wear a distinctive uniform. Have them direct traffic, curb hecklers, that sort of thing."

Bert looked over at the Field Marshal. He said, "It sounds like a good idea."

Van Eckmann said, "We've already formed two police forces in Elysium. One above board, and one secret, to root out subversives and other opponents of the State."

Karadja's smile was that of a carnivore again. "You're learning," he told them in approval.

His eyes went from one to the other. "Very well," he said. "I suggest that you step up your propaganda. Meanwhile, we shall see what an unkind fate has in store for your King Ford, your Susie and," he added, relishing it, "your Rex."

Chapter Thirteen

Susie, Virginia Dare and King Ford were staring at the Tri-Di screen in dismay. Balt sat to one side, boredom all over his teenaged face, and not bothering to look or listen.

Susie said, "It's been going on for over a week and each day it intensifies."

Virginia Dare said, "What surprises me is some of the people involved. Why, three of them are members of the Council. What it amounts to is they're advocating their own removal from control."

Balt snorted.

His mother looked over at him. "What's the matter, dear?"

Balt said lazily, "Never fear. If the Sons of Liberty ever took over, Bert, Jean and Lonzo would be represented in the ranks of the new super-super Council. In fact, I suspect that Bert would be the new High Councilor. Those original Sons of Liberty, back during the American Revolution, were the most liberated of all, after their side won out."

Susie looked over at him and said, "Why, Balt, you're absolutely cynical in your sophomoric wisdom."

He looked at her suspiciously. "Define sophomoric wisdom."

"It's something people of your age had back when I was a girl and schooling was somewhat different. I think it was Mark Twain who once wrote that at fifteen he was amazed how stupid his father was. And amazed again at how much his parent had learned by the time the son had reached his twenties."

"Very astute," Balt grunted. "However, wisdom isn't necessarily the prerogative of the elderly. If so, the great advances of the race would have been made by the old. With few exceptions, they weren't. Unfortunately, the old get ossified in the head as well as the body."

"Thank you, Balt," Susie said sweetly.

"Oh, I didn't mean you," he said, and for a contrite statement to come from Balt was a precedent.

The program had ended and King said, "They're increasing the tempo. Isn't there any way of damming it up? Who's in charge of your Communications? It seems to me that half the current broadcasts are from the Sons of Liberty. Aren't people getting bored with it?"

Susie said, "Forrest is Councilor of Communications. However, it would seem that the listeners aren't bored. It's something new. What they were bored with was what went before. This might not last long; the newness will wear off. But for now, it's something different."

Balt said, cynically again, "The newness won't have time to wear off. At the rate they're going, they'll demand their referendum one of these days and win it."

Martha wandered in from the kitchen, licking her fingers, and said, "There's a good comedy program on."

"Play it back later," King said glumly. "We just heard a comedy program and it's giving me ulcers."

Martha said, her tone petulant, "I can't imagine listening to speeches, they're so Zen-awful."

Susie said tartly, "It wouldn't hurt you to listen to some of these, dear, they'll probably affect the rest of your life."

She reached over and turned off the set, thinned her eyes and said thoughtfully, "You know, these speeches don't sound off the cuff, as the old expression had it. They sound as though there's somebody behind it all who knows propaganda from A to Z. It's a little too pat for people like Bert and Jean. Bert's admittedly a top man in Transport and Jean in Statistics, but they have no background in propaganda."

Martha said, her tone indicating she didn't really care, "What in the name of Zen is propaganda?"

"It means propagating your ideas. They don't necessarily have to be true or false, you're just trying to put them over. In times past, the term got a false image. People thought that propaganda meant lies. But, as an example, when Jesus was making with his parables and so forth, he was simply rendering his propaganda."

Balt murmured, "To render means to tear apart, doesn't it? Some of those parables . . ."

King ignored him and said, "Why doesn't your Councilor of Communications drop the old anchor on these Sons of Liberty? They're trying to subvert every institution Lagrangia is based upon."

And Susie said wearily, "One of those institutions, King, is freedom of speech."

The young man from the asteroids said, "But it comes back to the old saying, freedom of speech doesn't include standing up in a theatre and yelling Fire!"

"Why not?" Balt yawned. "Surely, freedom of speech is more important than losing a few theatres full of people, usually morons, from what I've seen of theatrical productions recently. Besides, the guy sitting next to him can always get up and yell, *He's a liar, there is no fire.*"

"Well, there's a fire here," Virginia Dare said in disgust.

King said, "I went to one of their rallies the other night. They actually had storm troopers standing around."

"What're storm troopers?" Martha said, still bored.

King glanced over at her and said, "You kids ought to read more Earthside history. Armed guards. They had clubs. They didn't have to use them often, but they had them handy, just in case. It kind of kept down any disagreement with the speakers."

Virginia Dare said to Susie, worry in her voice, "How are our own plans going?"

"Rather slowly," the older woman told her. "Forrest is going to speak later tonight, rebutting Bert's talk. And tomorrow Konstantin, the former Russian Nobel Prize winner. Both of them have considerable prestige among the rank and file Lagrangists."

"So has Bert," King said glumly. "The trouble is, the Sons of Liberty have a program and we haven't. It's a lousy program, from our viewpoint, but it's something definite. They claim they want to get the show back on the road and that a strong government is necessary to do it. Our speakers are stymied. They're faced with unemployment, a slow-down of the birth rate, and a falling off of emigration and we have no program to offer to reverse these trends. In fact, they're all getting worse."

Susie said, "Well, one plus factor is that most of the Council are with us. Bert, Jean, and Lonzo are definitely with the Sons of Liberty. Paul and Evelyn vacillate a little. But all the rest are with us and the Council carries a lot of weight in Lagrangia. We're going to hold a rally in Casey Park in a few days and all us anti-Sons of Liberty Councilors will be there to speak."

"You too?" Balt said.

She looked over at the boy, slumped in his chair, hands in pockets. "Me, too. I'm to be chairwoman."

King said suddenly, "By the way, where's Rex? He ought to be in on this bull session."

Susie said, "He's out taking his evening constitutional. He likes to keep in trim; walks a couple of miles or so every night."

"All alone?" King said sourly. "After some character took a shot at him?"

"Oh, it's unlikely that anything would happen right here in New Frisco."

But Susie was wrong.

Rex was striding along the nearly deserted streets of the suburbs of New Frisco. He walked briskly, enjoying the exercise, but his mind was on the problem of the Sons of Liberty and on the presence of Theodor Karadja in Grissom. He had no idea of how the two connected but he suspected that they did. It couldn't be coincidence that shortly after the Soviet agent's arrival in Lagrangia Bert and his Sons of Liberty launched their bid for power.

He strongly suspected that Karadja was in the background insofar as the Sons of Liberty were concerned. They were being too efficient, too professional about their rallies, parades, Tri-Di speeches and pamphlets. It was all going like clockwork. Bert—it had become obvious that Bert was the head of the movement—was a competent man but he had been a transportation engineer all of his life, not a rabble rouser. He and the other leaders of the revolutionists had never had occasion to indulge in politics or any other phase of socioeconomic activity. Jean was in Statistics and had probably never given a speech in her life to more than a handful of fellow workers. Lonzo, Councilor for Education, was another thing, but even he had probably never spoken in public to thousands of persons at a time.

No. Something off-beat was going on, and Rex and the others didn't have a clue. He suspected that the Lagrangists, with their traditions of freedom, if given a chance to vote on the Sons of Liberty at this point would turn it down. But the revolutionists were gaining ground. Out of sheer boredom, thousands of unemployed Lagrangists were joining up so that they could wear the striking new uniforms that had been devised by the Sons of Liberty. Also, they could participate in the parades, demonstrations and rallies. Sheer boredom can be a powerful force. How long would it be before the foe would decide they could swing the vote of a majority of the Lagrangists and call for a referendum?

He suspected that they couldn't wait too long. He who is bored is fickle. Try to hold his attention for too long and it wanders; he begins to look for other diversions to attract him.

Rex was on his return to the apartment and passing a park which was heavily shaded when the attack came. The only other people in sight at the time were a couple walking hand in hand perhaps a hundred meters before him.

He could hear the bike approaching from behind him but it didn't occur to Rex to turn and look. Bicyclists weren't exactly a rarity on the streets of New Frisco.

Suddenly, a burning, agonizing, tearing blow struck his right side and down he went toward the pavement of the sidewalk. Even as he fell, he recognized what had happened. He'd been hit, albeit glancingly, by a laser beam. A laser weapon in Lagrangia!

He fought the agony in desperate attempt to refrain from blacking out. The less than youthful bones of Rex Bader protested as he hit the cement. His every instinct was to seek cover, to roll to some protection, but there was no place to hide. The bole of the nearest tree was at least twelve feet away, though its branches extended over him.

He could hear the sounds of someone dismounting from a bicycle and then approaching to make sure he'd had it or to finish him off. A moving bicycle steered with one hand isn't the most stable firing platform known.

Even in the agony of the wound, Rex wanted to draw his own weapon but the shoulder harness was under him. He tried to roll and new pain swept over him. He could hear the sounds of the other's feet, approaching with care. Probably the assassin was acquainted with the fact that Rex Bader, though now an old man, had in his time been a pro.

Summoning every strength in his body, Rex lashed back with his right foot. It was an act of sheer desperation; he had not expected the kick to make contact.

But it did! He heard a yelp of surprise, a clattering of something metallic on the sidewalk and then a mutter of what were obviously curses in a language he didn't recognize.

Rex made a supreme agonizing effort, continued his roll and got his hand up to the holster. He pulled the Gyro-jet out, fumbled the safety off. He now could make out the other in the dimness of the Grissom night, darker still in the shade of the park's trees. His assailant was scrabbling around furiously on the ground, and Rex realized what had happened. The kick had caused the other to drop his pistol and he was having one hell of a time finding it.

The man looked at Rex in surprise from behind a tree, his face white in the night. And suddenly he gave up his efforts to find his own weapon, turned and sped away into the trees. Rex hadn't a clear shot and he doubted that he would have been able to make a hit in his present condition of pain and shock.

He lay there for a time, breathing deeply. He could feel the blood oozing from his side. He hadn't the vaguest idea of how badly he had been wounded, but he was still conscious, which was something.

Somehow, he managed to draw himself to his knees. He remained there, breathing deeply for another couple of minutes, and then, with another supreme effort, staggered to his feet. He should try to find the fallen laser gun, he knew, but also knew he'd never make it. The gun and abandoned bicycle would have to remain on the scene. He doubted that the assassin would return for them.

Slowly, clumsily, in deep pain, he began staggering toward the apartment. Thank the Holy Zen that it wasn't far. He had his right hand clasped to his side, stemming the flow of blood to the extent he could; but with his new exertions he could feel it now, running down as far as his thigh.

He had returned his gun to its holster and now continued to wobble on. Was it his imagination or was his sight beginning to fade? He shook his head in an effort to clear his vision.

He made it to the entry of the apartment but then looked at the stairs and shook his head again, this time in rejection. He could never stumble up those stairs to the third floor and there was no way of summoning assistance.

He stood there swaying and in despair, breathing deeply, and then finally sank to his knees and began crawling. His vision was fading again.

Inside the apartment, Balt, who was seated nearest to the door, looked over at it and scowled and said, "What in the hell's that?"

"What?" Martha said.

The others looked at him too.

He said, "I thought I heard a scratching sound from out in the hall."

"Imagination," Susie told him.

"No. There it is again."

King, scowling now as well, came to his feet, self-consciously loosened the Gyro-jet Rex had given him in its holster and went over to the door. He opened it carefully and stared down in horror.

"Give me a hand," he called. "It's Rex!"

The former detective was sprawled in the hallway in a gruesome puddle of blood.

Balt hurried forward and, between them, he and King manhandled the wounded Rex to a couch.

"A doctor!" Virginia Dare said shrilly, and headed for the TV phone on the desk.

But Rex got his eyes open and panted. "No. No, wait a . . . a minute."

"What do you mean!" Susie snapped. "You're hurt."

"Werner, Medicine Council. Is he one of ours?"

They were all staring at him.

Susie understood what he meant. "Yes," she said.

"Then send for him. But nobody else."

"But an ambulance, to get you to a hospital."

"No. Just get Werner," he panted. "Get me out of this jacket and shirt. Get my first aid kit from my sports things in my room. Then . . ."

But Rex Bader had passed out.

When he revived it was to find Werner, the most eminent doctor in Lagrangia, bent over him, his face worried. The others were gathered around, but at a respectful distance. When the doctor saw that the elderly Rex had revived, he said, "I've got to get you to the hospital for a transfusion and shots. You've got third-degree burns too, my friend. Laser cut, by the looks of it. If it hadn't partly cauterized its own wound you'd have bled to death by now."

Rex shook his head weakly. "No. Bring the stuff here. I can't leave the apartment."

The other glowered at him in exasperation. "Why not?"

Rex looked at Susie. "Can't you see? If it gets out that I've been nailed in a street shootout, it gives the Sons of Liberty another weapon. They can claim that the streets of Grissom aren't safe. They're already calling for a police force, under their control."

His eyes went weakly to King. "Go down to Druid Park. You'll find a bicycle lying there in the street.

Near it, somewhere on the sidewalk, is a laser pistol. Go get it before somebody else finds it. And King—" The younger man was already at the door but turned. "Keep that Gyro-Jet handy." Then the old man passed out.

Chapter Fourteen

By the time King got back from Druid Park with the laser pistol, Rex was comfortably ensconced in his bed, taking plasma. A mystified attendant had brought the equipment from the hospital and it had been taken from him at the door.

Balt and Martha had left, after being thoroughly briefed by Susie as to the necessity of complete secrecy. Though both were somewhat wide-eyed, they agreed. Obviously, neither of them had ever seen the results of a shooting before. Even more sobering, the victim was a person they knew well.

Just before they left, Martha had swallowed and whispered to Susie, "Is he going to . . . die?"

"No, of course not," the older woman had replied quickly, but as she returned to the bedroom she was inwardly praying to gods she didn't believe in that her reassurance was valid.

Virginia Dare, King, and Werner were gathered around the bed when Susie came in.

The doctor was saying, "I still think we ought to

get you to the hospital where you'll get proper care."

"No," the wounded man said, shaking his head. "I've been hit worse than this."

"Possibly. Back when you were a young man. But somebody of your years doesn't heal so easily. You should have nurses on a round-the-clock basis."

"No! The fewer who know about this, the better. I have a suspicion that this was deliberately set up to give the Sons of Liberty something to trumpet about."

Susie said, "It's hard to believe that Bert . . ."

"Maybe it wasn't Bert. Where in the name of Zen would any of his people get a laser pistol?"

The doctor said, "No more talk." He looked at Susie and Virginia Dare. "I want somebody here in this room with him at all times. I'll return in the morning, unless I'm called sooner."

Susie said to Virginia Dare, "I'll take over for the night. You go get some sleep." She looked from the girl to King. "Do you two have something going?" When they both nodded, she said, "Good."

As they left the apartment building, Virginia Dare said to him, "My place, or yours?"

"It had better be yours," he told her unhappily. "Both that Soviet Complex operative and the five Elitists from Elysium are at my hotel. If they've got to the point where they're shooting Lagrangist celebrities, just to stir up controversy, they might take a shot at you. You're even better known than Rex is."

She accepted it. "All right," she said as they got bikes.

As they pedalled out into the hills toward Heidi, he growled, "Damn it, we aren't getting anywhere. I've been here a couple of weeks and I still haven't a clue to what the Elitists are up to. Why in the hell did they come here from Elysium?"

She shook her head and said, "Overnight, Lagrangia has turned from Utopia to a frightening hell. In all of my life, I have never heard of anyone being shot in Grissom. I have never heard of anything like this bunch of Sons of Liberty goons you called storm troopers. I have never heard of any sizeable group recommending any sort of government here that wasn't as pure a democracy as the human race has ever seen."

"Well, you're hearing it now," he said grimly.

They approached Heidi and as they rode down the main street, passing the *gasthaus* where the revelry seemed even more than usual, King said suddenly, "What do you say we go in and have a nightcap? Aside from the drink, I wouldn't mind listening in to barroom conversation. Probably a lot of them will be talking about the Sons of Liberty."

"Wizard," she said. "I could use a drink. They have excellent *dunkles* beer here. A special brew. They brought the recipe up from Switzerland."

They parked the bikes and entered the large barroom of the *gasthaus*.

Similar to Susie's house, a Swiss motif was maintained. King had never before seen the Swiss version of a tavern, save on Tri-Di shows, but he realized that it must be as authentic as could possibly be realized. There was a three-piece orchestra, consisting of zither, accordion and violin, the musicians all done up in authentic Swiss mountaineer's garb, and two harried bartenders similarly dressed behind the heavy pseudo-wood bar, industriously serving some thirty or forty thirsty customers. Some of these were standing, some at the thick pseudo-wood tables which had benches rather than chairs.

King was unhappily surprised to see that almost half of the men and women present wore the Sons of Liberty uniform.

They took a small table near one of the windows that faced out on the street and a scurrying wait-ress, all smiles and wearing a dirndl dress, took their order for two steins of dark beer.

King said, "I'm surprised that you Lagrangists employ live labor in a place like this. All bars are automated in the Promised Land Islands."

She laughed. "You're still pushed for labor, out there," she told him. "But these people aren't employees."

He eyed her in puzzlement, frowned and then looked over at the bartenders and the band. "What are you talking about?"

"It's voluntary labor. A hobby. A club. Practi-cally everybody in town belongs to it. We take turns acting as bartenders, waitresses and all the rest. Of course, it isn't obligatory to take your turn but there're always more volunteers than jobs. It's fun. I've acted as barmaid here several times. I can draw a wizzard mug of beer."

Everybody in the barroom seemed to know Virginia Dare. They waved, called over to her but seeing King, a stranger, they stayed where they were, deducing that the pair wished to be alone.

When their beer came, they sipped and King tried to make out some of the conversation in their vicinity. He had been right. A great deal of the talk dealt with the controversy between the Sons of Liberty and the old hands who opposed them. They seemed to be about equally divided, so far as King could make out, which was depressing. The enemy was getting his message across.

Suddenly, he put his hand out and on her arm. "Did you see that?" he blurted.

"See what?"

"Those two men who just rode past the window. I'd swear that one of them was Theodor Karadja. Come on!" He came to his feet and headed for the door.

"Who?" she said, as they came out onto the main street.

"Karadja, the Soviet Complex espionage man that Dale Mickoff warned Rex about. He showed us a picture of him. I'm sure that was one of the men going down the street there. Let's go!" He hurried toward their bikes.

She followed, saying, mystified, "But what do you expect to do, King?"

"I don't know," he said hurriedly as they climbed on their wheels. "But perhaps we can figure out what they're up to."

"One of them lives here in Heidi. His name's Stanley. He has a little house of his own and lives alone. Well, except when, once in awhile, he has a girl with him for a time. Usually he's a loner. Never comes to the *gasthaus*, for instance.''

He thought about that. ''Then the other one is Karadja. They must be heading for this Stanley's house. That means we don't have to stick so close to them that they might spot us. If that espionage man is as sharp as Rex seems to think, he'd probably notice a tail, particularly amateurs such as us.''

They allowed the couple in front of them to disappear down the street.

''Wizard,'' King said. ''Now, let's go to this Stanley's house.''

''What will we do there?''

''I don't know. But I'm armed. I've even got the laser pistol Rex was wounded with. Can you shoot?''

''No, of course not.'' She shivered in rejection. ''Stanley's house is up this side street, the third house up.''

''Wizard. Let's leave the bikes here and walk the rest of the way. We'll be able to stay in the shadows better.''

They put the bikes in the nearest rack and headed up the narrow cobblestoned street with care.

Shortly, Susie indicated a small house with, ''That's Stanley's place.''

The house was set back from the street aways and was somewhat similar to that of Virginia Dare's. There was a considerable expanse of lawn around it. Two bicycles were leaning up against the front, next to the door and there was a single lighted room, curtains drawn.

''Only two bikes,'' King said in a whisper, hardly

called for considering the distance. "So there's probably only the two of them. I wonder what in Zen they're up to."

"I wish Uncle Rex hadn't been shot," she said. "He'd know what to do. But I wouldn't even want to call him. He's probably asleep."

"Yeah," he said. He looked at her. His own complexion was so dark that it would be difficult to see him in the blackness of the night, but Virginia Dare's fine, pale features were clear even in the dimness.

King said, "Can you whistle?"

"Of course."

"All right. You stay here in the shadow of this other house. If anybody comes, start whistling. Anything, just so it's loud enough for me to hear."

"What are you going to do?"

"I don't know. Scout around. If I'm not back in a half hour, you hurry to Susie's place and tell them what happened."

"Oh, King, are you sure you know what you're doing? These are very bad . . ."

"Don't I know it?" he said grimly. "But my father and the Committee didn't send me here to sit around in hotels and restaurants. I'll see you, darling."

He disappeared into shadows.

A little later, she thought she saw a dark figure ghosting across the lawn of the Stanley house.

Aside from children's games, at which he had been exceptionally good, King Ford had never had occasion to skulk about houses. Happily, this was the only house in the vicinity that was lighted up. It would seem that the others nearby were either unoccupied or the tenants were away from home—possibly at the *gasthaus*.

He circled the place completely, at a distance. Then closing in, choosing the darkest area behind the residence, he flitted into the shadows of the wall. He had spotted a rear door, probably leading into the cottage's kitchen. Now he placed his ear against it for long moments, without result.

He brought forth his Gyro-jet, trying to remember what Rex had told him about the gun's operation. To date, he still hadn't fired the piece. Their lessons in its operation had been thwarted out in the wilderness by the sniper. He recalled the safety stud and flicked it off, dismayed by its audible snick.

He took a deep breath and tried the door knob. As usual on Grissom, the door was unlocked. The room beyond was dark and, he assumed, empty. He entered, leaving the door behind him open for a quick retreat. On the opposite side of the room, a faint sliver of light showed from beneath another door. Slowly, silently, he made his way in that direction. Mentally he kept his fingers crossed. All he needed to do was to stumble into some piece of furniture and create a noise. He did bump into a chair, but so slowly was he moving that he managed to avoid sound.

At the door, once again he pressed his ear to it. He could hear voices beyond but not make out what was being said. *Damn.*

Well, there was no other choice; he had to take his chances, having come this far. If either of the two beyond were looking in the direction of the door, he'd had it.

With ultimate quiet, he put his left hand down to the knob, his gun at the ready in his right. He twisted infinitely slowly, and then gently pushed until the door was open the merest crack.

They were speaking in Russian.

King Ford read Russian better than he spoke or understood it. As a student, besides Interlingua he had studied English, French and Russian, since he wanted to read the literature in the original. Translations had always irritated him. Happily, his school years were not that far behind him. He could follow this, though not too very well.

One voice was saying, "I'd rather you not be in on this, Comrade Shvets. I suggest that you go on into your bedroom until I recall you."

And the other voice said, "Yes, Comrade Major."

King could hear a door open and close. He assumed that Comrade Major was Theodor Karadja and that the other was one of his underlings, the man Virginia Dare had called Stanley and whose real name was evidently Shvets. He took another chance and pushed the door open to the point that he could get an eye to the crack.

The room beyond, lit by a single old-fashioned Swiss table lamp, held one person who sat at a desk, his back to King Ford. King pressed the door open slightly further, the better to hear and observe. He hadn't the vaguest idea of what was going on.

Karadja, and King could make just enough of the agent's profile to know that it was him indeed, was saying, "This is Theodor Karadja. I wish to speak to Minister Kurancheva. Scrambled, of course."

From where he was stationed, King couldn't hear the reply.

After a full minute or more, the Soviet agent said, "Wladyslaw? This is Theodor. I thought I'd better give you a progress report."

King had hit the jackpot. He let air out of his lungs, in gratitude at his luck.

He still could hear nothing of the other end of the conversation. Undoubtedly, the Soviet operative was talking to an Earthside superior. And, yes, now it came to him. The other had asked for Minister Kuranchev and had then called him Wladyslaw.

Wladyslaw Kurancheva. Even in the far asteroid belt, the notorious right-hand man of Number One, and the ultimate head of the Soviet Complex secret police, was known. This must be very big indeed, if Karadja was reporting to him direct. King strained his ears, desperately tried to remember his Russian.

Karadja was saying, "Matters are progressing satisfactorily. The leaders of the so-called Sons of Liberty are incredibly naive. They hang on my words when I give them advice on their program and methods of propaganda. We have bugged various of their meeting places as well as the homes of Bert, Jean, and Lonzo. Also the two suites of the Elitists from Elysium. They are stupid in matters pertaining to conspiracy, but since their opposition is just as naive it is not important; in fact it will undoubtedly be in our favor. In their stupidity, they expect to betray us, once they have come to power."

The espionage agent held silence for a moment and then went on. "Yes, Wladyslaw we shall see who betrays whom when the sticking point comes. Their opposition is led by most of the members of their Council and by Rex Bader. A quarter of a century ago, in cooperation with Comrade Ilya Simonov who was then still active in the ministry, Bader thwarted the efforts of the oil cartels of the time to sabotage Lagrangia. The success of Bader and Simonov led to the Lagrange Five declaration of independence from the Reunited Nations. At that time the Central Committee supported the steps, now to our sorrow."

He paused, then said, his voice contrite, "Yes, of course, Wladyslaw—no, I would not patronize you, I was but recapitulating. At any rate, this Rex Bader, in spite of his age, is undoubtedly the most dangerous of our opponents. He and Doctor Susie Hawkins, formerly the secretary of Professor Casey, are both dangerous. Secondary to them are King Ford, from the Asteroid Federation, and Virginia Dare."

Another pause and then, "She is popular as a result of the fact that she was the first child born in space. The Lagrangists love her—yes, as you say, as a mascot of sorts—and she is in a position to swing votes when the referendum is called for. We decided to make an attempt on Rex Bader both to remove him from the scene and to stir up controversy. The fool Frol Pogodin was given the assignment of shooting him down on the street. He made a botch of it and though he undoubtedly wounded the old man, we don't know how badly."

Karadja listened some more and then said, "We don't know. Thus far, the Sons of Liberty have stolen a march on the opposition but Rex Bader, Susie Hawkins, and their adherents are beginning to gather their strength. They are to hold a special mass rally in a few days. Meanwhile, I have moved from my quarters in the hotel in New Frisco and gone into hiding in the home of Vadim Shvets. Without doubt, by this time my identity has become known and they would soon discover where I was residing."

He paused for a response and then said, "Yes, of course, Comrade Kurancheva."

King shifted his weight and one of his knee joints clicked softly.

The Rumanian flicked off whatever device he was utilizing and sat unmoving for a moment as though in thought.

Suddenly his hand flung out, viper fast, and dashed the sole lighted lamp of the room to the floor. The lamp shattered, leaving the living room in darkness.

King Ford, completely taken by surprise, froze there at the crack of the door.

Then he could hear a scurrying movement. In a confusion at the unexpected development, he tightened his finger on the gun's trigger and two shots ripped from the Gyro-jet. He had no idea whatever where either of them went. He spun clumsily and dashed for the kitchen door, careening off the same chair he had hit before and this time not so gently.

Behind him, the living room door banged open.

Even as he sped out onto the back lawn, he could hear, or imagined he heard, the hiss of a laser beam.

He dashed to the right, to get out of the line of fire as quickly as possible, and around the corner of the house. He was thanking the stars that he had involuntarily fired his gun. Now, at least, his pursuers would know that he was armed and might be cautious in the pursuit.

He headed at full speed for where he had left Virginia Dare, expecting momentarily to be hit between his shoulder blades and to be hit far worse than had Rex. He was in excellent physical trim and ran with the speed of an athlete. He had no compunction whatsoever about retreat. There were two of the enemy and one of him, and they were seasoned veterans at this sort of thing.

He gasped to Virginia Dare when he came up to her, "Quick, they're after us. You must know this town better than either of them. Get us to your house by back ways. We'll have to shake them on the way. I don't think that either of them really got a look at me."

Chapter Fifteen

Balt, Martha, Jim and Tom slouched in chairs in the office of the president of the Young People's 150 Club. There was an open box of trank pills on the desk but none of them had taken more than one. They were too far caught up in what they were involved in to want to run the chance of becoming over-tranked. Stimulation can go so far and then you're over the precipice.

Balt said to Jim, "Well, how goes the Hunting Club?"

"Wizard. Right in the old vulva."

Martha snorted beneath her breath.

Balt looked at Tom. "And the Karate and Judo Club?"

"So far so good. We located an old fart who used to have a black belt in karate, down Earthside. He's unemployed now, of course, along with everybody else, so he was pleased as a pig in shit to take on training us dizzard kids in how to kill your fellow man by kicking him in the balls and such."

Balt said, in the way of report, "And all's clear on the Sons of Liberty front. Bert liked the idea of having a youth auxiliary so much that I'm considered not just the head of the Youth Auxiliary but I sit in on most of the meetings of their higher echelons."

"Most?" Jim said, rubbing his prominent nose.

"Yeah," Balt told him. "Even when they're conferring with these twats from Elysium. By the way, I thought the asteroid belt Islands had the same requirements for colonists as Lagrangia. That is, a minimum I.Q. of 130. But if some of those so-called Elitists from Elysium are up to the minimum, I surrender. The I.Q. tests aren't valid."

Tom said, "Well, we're all acquainted with the story of Elysium. Settled by anarchists. From what I've read, there was never an anarchist to come down the track who'd stand for *any* kind of requirement."

"At any rate," Balt said. "I sit in on all the upper echelon meetings except when a certain Pierre Cannes shows up. He's Mister Mystery Man and neither a Lagrangist nor from the asteroid belt. With a name like that, he should be French but he isn't. He doesn't ever speak Interlingua and when he talks with Bert or the others it's in English; English with a slight accent that I'd say came from East Europe."

"Oh, oh," Jim said. "The Soviet Complex?"

Balt nodded. "That'd be my guess. I know for one thing that Bert is using tactics that I doubt he came up with on his own. There's somebody with experience in these things and it must be this Pierre Cannes. Another thing: Rex was shot with a laser.

Nobody in Lagrangia had a laser pistol. How he smuggled it in, I don't know. But I suspect that our Pierre Cannes is the gunman."

"Oh, wizard," Tom said in disgust. "First we're opposed to the conventional Lagrangists, then we're opposed to the Sons of Liberty, and now we've got the Soviet Complex to contend with. What do we do now, Balt?"

"I don't know. We play it by ear. The trouble is, the Sons of Liberty are right."

The other three eyed him.

He said, "The Council and Rex and Susie's group are doing just what Bert and his followers contend. Nothing. Lagrangia is going to pot and they're doing nothing about it."

"Then why don't we really join up with the Sons of Liberty, not just pretend to be a youth auxiliary?" Martha said.

He looked over at her. "Because our secret program has been to keep together until we're old enough and large enough in numbers to take over ourselves, by whatever means we figure out when the time comes. But if the Sons of Liberty get in, the first thing they'll do is change the rules so that nobody will ever be able to get them out again. And we'll have had it. In Elysium, one of the first things the Elitists did when they got into power was to start up a police, both ordinary and secret. Don't think for a moment that Bert won't do the same. He and Jean and Lonzo have already made some preliminary steps in that direction."

He shook his head in disgust. "The situation doesn't augur very well for us."

Martha looked at him and snorted. "Augur, yet. You're using mighty fancy words these days, fella."

Balt grinned and said, "Knock, knock."

She groaned but said, "Who's there?"

"Augur."

"Augur who?"

"Augur screw yourself."

She pretended indignation. "What? With three perfectly healthy cloddies around?"

Balt stood and said, "I think I'll go over and see how Rex is making out. Putting him out of action was a good move on the part of that Soviet agent, or whoever did it. Rex was the nearest thing that we have in Lagrangia to somebody knowledgeable about this kind of razzle. Now he's out of the running."

Jim stood too, bobbed his Adam's apple a couple of times and said, "Yeah, and I've got a get-together of the Young People's Hunting Club arranged out in the wilderness."

Balt said to him, "They've all got guns by now?"

"Oh, sure. We've all had guns for over a week. No trouble at all. The distribution center didn't murmur when we applied for them under the name of the club. Same thing applied in the other Islands when our local groups applied. Each club member has a .22 hunting rifle and a .22 target pistol."

"Twenty-two?" Balt said unhappily. "Couldn't you get a larger caliber than that?"

Jim said, "Possibly, but it might look a little strange if a bunch of kids applied for heavier calibers. Besides, there's nothing wrong with a .22

Long Rifle cartridge. It's where you hit a target more than what you hit him with."

Balt shrugged off his disagreement and said to Martha, "Coming?"

"No," she said. "I hate to see sick people. Gives me the blue spiders." She added, wickedly, "Besides, there was something I wanted to talk to Tom about."

Balt grunted at that and cast an eye in disfavor of Tom.

That worthy spread his hands in a gesture of appeal. "I didn't say anything."

Balt and Jim walked out of the building together and took up bikes.

Jim said, disconsolately, "It doesn't look so good, does it?"

"No," Balt told him. "It doesn't. What it amounts to is that we don't want either the present Council nor the Sons of Liberty to head Lagrangia. And we're not old enough to take over ourselves. Adults wouldn't stand for a bunch of kids from fifteen to twenty taking over the reins of government. They wouldn't realize that we could probably do a better job of it."

They were heading in opposite directions, so waved a brisk goodbye and separated.

The president of the Young People's 150 Club tried to come up with some plans as he made his way to the apartment where Rex was bedridden. But he couldn't surface an idea. He considered revealing the whole thing to Rex and Susie and offering to team up with them in an effort to thwart the Sons of Liberty. The scenario lacked appeal.

Suppose that they were successful and the Council remained in power for the next five years or so, until the Club 150 was ready to make its bid. In five years, the way things were going, Lagrangia could be a shambles, not worth taking over.

He pulled up before his destination and entered the apartment building and started up the stairs to the third floor. Just before entering the apartment his face took on his habitual bored cynicism and he slouched in, hands in his pockets.

Susie, King and Virginia Dare were all in Rex's bedroom, where the old man was propped up with pillows, looking pale and weak. For that matter, Susie looked tired as well. She'd had only two hours sleep, after Virginia Dare and King had appeared on the scene. They had spent the night in Heidi, afraid to return to the city until daylight. Though they thought they had shaken the two Soviet Complex agents, they couldn't be sure.

When Balt entered, Susie was sitting at the room's desk, checking something out on the TV phone screen. He slumped into a chair without speaking, so as not to interrupt her. The others were looking on the serious side, even for this gathering.

She finally turned and said, "As an honorary member of the Council, I was able to get his Dossier Complete from the data banks. There was no difficulty at all, in view of the fact that Virginia Dare was able to give the location of the house he occupies. That, of course, was in the data banks. His name is Stanley M-E-A-99-GR2398 and he was born in Ireland under the name Stanley Ryan in 1999. He came to Lagrangia about five years ago as an elec-

trical engineer and has been unemployed since the
Island Five project was discontinued."

"What else?" Rex got out with an effort.

"Precious little else," Susie told him. "So little,
for instance, about his life Earthside before he
sought employment in Lagrange Five that I suspect
his documents are forged. I've never seen such a
sparse Dossier."

Rex said musingly, "Just for routine, we can call
Dale Mickoff and get him to check it through his
Inter-American Bureau of Investigation. Not that it
makes much difference. We know he's a Soviet
Complex agent and now that his cover has been
blown he'll go to ground. I have no doubt that there
are other Soviet operatives in Grissom. They'll hide
him out. Possibly, he'll be sent to one of the other
Islands."

Virginia Dare said indignantly, "But he'll never
get out of Lagrange Five to return Earthside. He'd
have to use his identification to take passage and
we can have the Transportation Function looking
for him."

"Possibly he doesn't want to leave Lagrangia,"
Susie said wryly. "Particularly after blowing his
cover. I understand that the Soviet espionage people take a dim view of failure."

"It wasn't really he who flubbed it," King said.
"It was Karadja himself when he allowed himself
to be spotted."

"What in the name of Zen are you all talking
about?" Balt said, yawning.

His mother turned to him and said, "Last night,
King and I went out to Heidi and by pure chance

spotted Theodor Karadja with another man I've known for years as Stanley. We followed them to Stanley's house and through sheer courage and . . ." she looked at King ". . . outrageous luck, King was able to sneak in and overhear most of a report Karadja was making, it would seem, to a superior, Earthside. He was detected—the man must have the senses of a hunted animal—but King was able to escape and we managed to get to our house and hide."

"I'll be a dizzard," Balt said, looking at King with new respect but as though he couldn't believe it of the other. "But who's this Karadja cloddy?"

Susie said, "Oh, we didn't tell you about him, did we? Rex got a call from Dale Mickoff of the IABI, Earthside. He warned us that Theodor Karadja of Soviet espionage, one of their most efficient operatives, was in Lagrangia, for what reason he didn't know. He goes under the name of Pierre Cannes and is staying at the Lagrange Hilton, or at least he was until last night."

"Pierre Cannes?" Balt said. "Damn, so that's who he is."

They turned curious gazes on him.

He shifted his shoulders slightly and said, "He's hand in glove with the Sons of Liberty. I think he's their big brain when it comes to spreading their message."

Rex said, "How'd you find that out?"

Balt said, an edge of defiance in his voice, "I've been working on this too, you know. I've spotted him several times with Bert, and Jean and Lonzo."

King says, "That bears out what I heard in Heidi.

The only heartening thing Karadja mentioned in his report was the fact that both the Sons of Liberty and Karadja distrust each other. Each expects to betray the other at some future date when they are no longer in mutual need." Remembering the Rumanian's quickness he added, "Karadja would eat them for breakfast."

Rex said, with an effort, "From now on we've got to intensify our self defense. He's onto us and now that he knows he was overheard, he can't afford to let us continue to operate."

King said defensively, "I don't think he spotted me. He doesn't know who was listening in."

Rex's voice was tired. "Like hell he doesn't. The sonofabitch is the top hatchetman for Wladyslaw Kurancheva. And you and Susie and Virginia Dare were lumped together with me, in his report to Moscow. Wizard. There are only two groups in Grissom who might try to spy on him, our group and the Sons of Liberty. And he's still necessary to Bert and his organization so they wouldn't take the chance of antagonizing him. That leaves us. And since he knows I'm out of the running, even if I was of age to be prowling around houses, you're the only one remaining. The fact that you fired a Gyrojet a couple of times at him also eliminates the Sons of Liberty. He might suspect that I have such weapons on hand, from the old days, but he knows damn well that other Lagrangists wouldn't have them."

"What can we do?" Virginia Dare said.

Rex drew a deep painful breath. "First of all, you can all move in here. We've got three weapons now, my two pistols and the laser we liberated from whoever shot me. Don't even go back to your home, or, King, you to the hotel."

"I'll have to get my things," King told him.

"And Balt and me too," Virginia Dare said.

But Susie backed Rex. "Oh, no, you don't," she said. "We can order anything you need, right from here, from the distribution center."

"Not me," Balt said. "From what you say, I'm not on the shit list. I have to be free to operate."

"Don't be ridiculous," Susie snapped at him. "You're young but you're not that young. And you're the son of Virginia Dare. They could get at her through you. And don't think they've got the scruples not to do just that. This Sons of Liberty movement becomes more opportunistic as it grows, and it's growing by leaps and bounds. They even have a uniformed Youth Auxiliary now."

It came out before Balt could catch himself. He couldn't keep from showing off in his usual arrogant manner when with his elders.

"Like hell they have," he said.

Virginia Dare frowned at him. "Susie's right, darling. This youth auxiliary has been organized for more than a week."

He couldn't back down now. "I know it has," he said. "But it's not necessarily theirs. It's composed of members of the 150 Club. We're careful not to let anybody else in. On one excuse or the other, we keep out anybody except club members."

"The 150 Club?" King said.

Virginia Dare looked over to him and said, "It's a club Balt belongs to. In fact, you're the president this year, aren't you dear? It's sort of a snobbish thing, if you ask me. The big requirement for joining is that you have an I.Q. exceeding 150."

Susie rolled her eyes upward, in pretended appeal to high powers, and said, "Homo Superior again."

"At any rate," Balt said. "We've infiltrated the Sons of Liberty."

Chapter Sixteen

Rex, Susie, King and Virginia Dare were holding a last council of war before the latter three took off for the rally in Casey Park at the soccer field there.

Rex said, "Damn, but I wish I could go. Imagine being flat on my butt at a time like this."

They looked at him unhappily.

Susie said, "What was Werner's opinion?"

Rex said, "I'm considerably better but he just laughed when I suggested I could make it to the rally."

"Wizard. Then that's that," King said definitely. "The better care you take of yourself, the sooner you'll be up and around." He hesitated, then said, "I'm worried about you being left here alone. How do we know that Karadja or Stanley won't show up and . . . give you a working over?"

Rex reached under his pillow and brought forth the Gyro-jet and put it atop the bedsheet, ready to his hand. He reached under the pillow again and came up with the laser pistol and put it to the other side of him.

He said grimly, "I wish the hell they'd try. I'd cut down the odds a little. But it won't happen. By this time, Karadja's found some manner of checking out how badly I was hit. He's not silly enough to expose himself to my fire if he tried to break in. No, I'm all right. It's you I'm worried about."

He looked at Susie. "I suggest that you phone for a hovercar and the three of you go to the park in it."

Susie frowned at that and said, "It wouldn't look good to the crowd. Kind of ostentatious. Everybody else, even the Council, will be coming on bikes."

"The hell with what it looks like," Rex said. "You're target number one for these bastards." He turned his eyes to King. "You'll be riding shotgun," he said. "When the car comes, all three of you go down to the lobby. Then, King, you go out, your hand on your Gyro-jet under your coat. Check up and down the street. Then open the car doors. Susie and Virginia Dare, you two make a run for it then; pile and get going soonest. Our hover cars will by no means stop a laser beam, so the sooner you're out of sight of anybody who might be staked out there, the better. Once you get to Casey Park, you should be safe. Too many people around for them to attempt a hit. Anybody trying it would be torn apart. You two are the most popular women in Lagrangia."

Virginia Dare looked at her wrist chronometer. "I suppose we should get going," she said. "The Council is to meet us at the speaker's stand."

Susie said, "Yes, and we shouldn't be late. The

Tri-Di news people might want some quick preliminary interviews. I suspect that ninety-nine percent of all Lagrangia will either be at the rally or, if they live in other Islands, or figure the park will be too packed, be stationed at their Tri-Di sets. This will undoubtedly be the biggest turn-out since we declared our independence from the Reunited Nations."

King said, "Yeah, and it ought to swing it. The right arm of Professor Casey, the patron saint of Lagrange Five, if the Lagrangists were religiously inclined: that's you, Susie, Casey's right arm. Then, all of the Council save three. And those Councilors were all democratically elected. Save for yourself, they're the most popular people, in each of their respective functions, in Island Three." He turned his eyes to Virginia Dare. "And the first true Lagrangist, Virginia Dare, the first child born in space."

He looked back to Rex. "How can it miss?"

Rex growled, "I don't know, but the enemy has been ominously quiet these past few days. They must have *something* in mind. But go on, all of you, get the hell out of here. I want to start watching this on the Tri-Di. Undoubtedly, the park's already crammed."

They trooped out.

In the Conference Room of the Administration Building of Grissom, seventeen of the Councilors were seated at the heavy metal table, most of them fidgeting.

Paul said, "Where in the hell are Bert, Lonzo and Jean? We ought to get this confounded meeting underway. We've got to get out to the park. What was the purpose of calling it, anyway?"

"Possibly Bert, Jean and Lonzo deliberately stayed away," Li said. "They know that the rest of us are all opposed to their Sons of Liberty and that following the meeting we'll all go to the rally and speak against them. Even Paul and Evelyn have now sided with the rest of us."

Forrest said, "Possibly. We'll just have to go on without them. Now, as Paul said, What *was* the purpose of this special meeting?"

They looked back and forth at each other.

Evelyn, of Art, said, "Why, I thought Werner summoned it. One of his secretaries called me and said we were to convene an hour before going to the rally."

The head of the Medical Function looked at her blankly. "You must be mistaken."

Li said, "I thought Paul called it. One of his assistants notified me."

Forrest, his face dark, came to his feet. "Okay; quickly, now," he said. "Who called this special meeting?"

There was empty silence.

"There's something devious here, and I don't like it," Paul said. "It's a trick. We're due out at Casey Park at any time. Dammit, we should be there now."

Jerry, of Research, a silent type who seldom spoke up at Council meetings and who didn't look like the towering scientist he had often proven himself to be, rasped, "Bert and his people aren't here. Something's up!"

And a smooth voice said, "Yes, it is."

From the three doors that led into the Conference Room, eight men entered. All wore stocking masks, all carried vicious looking hand weapons.

The one who had spoken, now said, his voice projecting friendliness, "Ah, shall we say that you are all under . . . temporary arrest?"

"What in the name of Zen is all this?" Forrest blurted.

The eight deployed themselves about the room, particularly covering the doors.

The spokesman said, "Suffice to say that this instrument in my hand is a laser pistol, as illegal, so I understand, in Lagrangia as it is anywhere in the, ah, civilized world."

"I don't believe it," Evelyn snapped. "There is no such thing in Lagrangia."

"My dear, how naive you are," the intruder told her.

He stepped closer to the table, activated the weapon and very neatly sheered off a corner. It dropped to the floor with a metallic clank.

It couldn't be seen through his textile mask, but obviously from the tone of his voice, he was beaming.

"Now truly," he said. "We have no desire to do any of you bodily harm. Though . . ." he paused ". . . if necessary that will be done. However, we do wish to keep you here for a couple of hours."

Forrest said, "You cloddy. You think that you can keep us from attending the Casey Park rally."

And the other said, "I *know* that I can, Councilor. Believe me, your life depends on it."

Paul said inanely, "You'll never get away with this."

And the gunman said politely, "Of course not. Meanwhile, I assume that none of you are armed. However, in your excitement you might consider, particularly you younger men, physical violence. Please don't. I told you that we don't desire to do any of you bodily injury—but we don't truly mind."

"What in the hell are you doing here with those silly masks and those dangerous guns?" Forrest got out indignantly.

"As I said, enjoying your company for a couple of hours during which, otherwise, you might have made dizzards of yourselves," the other told him.

"You're mad," Evelyn got out. "Things like this simply can't happen in Lagrangia."

He turned his masked face to her. "Alas, dear lady, but for the immediate future I am afraid that you will see more and more of it. Then, of course, all this turmoil will settle down." He added dryly, "I assume."

Paul said heatedly, "Obviously, you're affiliated with the Sons of Liberty. As soon as you let us go, we'll immediately go on Tri-Di and reveal how we were kept from attending the rally."

The spokesman of the gunmen laughed softly. "Who'd believe you?" he said. "Come now, it's an unlikely story, on the face of it. You'll contend that eight masked men, armed with laser pistols, forced you to remain here. But there are no laser pistols in Grissom and there hasn't been a crime of violence in a quarter of a century of more. The Sons of Liberty will indignantly deny the whole story and contend that you, ah, chickened out, as the old Americanism has it."

Evelyn blurted, "You're speaking English, rather than Interlingua. You're no Lagrangist."

He waggled the laser pistol in her direction. "That'll be all," he said. "No more talking."

In Casey Park, next to the speaker's stand, Susie looked up and down worriedly. She said, "Where in the name of Zen can the Council be? It's long past time for the meeting to begin."

King bit his lower lip and told them, "The Tri-Di boys are getting teed off."

And Virginia Dare said, "This is unbelievable. The idea was that we'd meet fifteen minutes before starting, so that we could decide on who'd speak in what order, that sort of thing. And here it is, fifteen minutes after the scheduled beginning."

One of the newsmen came up and said, "How about it, Susie? We've used up all the time we can, scanning the crowds and so on." He indicated the teeming tens of thousands of Lagrangists who packed the soccer field. A good many of them were muttering impatiently and some were calling out from time to time to get things moving.

King muttered, "We're losing votes by the minute."

Susie said to the Tri-Di man, "I simply don't know what to say, Dalton. I have no idea what's holding up the Council."

Dalton said, respect battling the impatience in his voice, "Look, Susie, why don't you get up there and start it off? Go into your chairwoman's speech.

They'll probably show up before you're through. If
they haven't, then introduce Virginia Dare, here,
and let her go into her talk. Surely, they'll be here,
or at least some of them, before she's done."

Susie sighed. She looked at Virginia Dare and
said wanly, "I suppose that's all we can do."

Followed by her younger companion, she
mounted the speaker's stand, and while Virginia
took one of the folding chairs, approached the mike.

She held up her hands in appeal for quiet and
said, "For some reason, most of our speakers
haven't as yet appeared."

"They've copped out!" someone from the audience jeered.

"No, of course that's not it," Susie said definitely. "We'll start the meeting and soon . . ."

"I'll bet they're over at the Sons of Liberty headquarters, joining up!" another heckler yelled.

That was followed by a wave of laughter going
through the restless crowd.

Someone else called, "Shut up! Let's hear what
Susie has to say."

Susie began, "Lagrangia is going through a
period of crisis and uncertainty."

A heckler called, "Damn right, the Council got us
into the mess."

King, standing down below, looked over at the
man, who wore one of the Sons of Liberty uniforms.
Undoubtedly, their membership was present in
numbers and spotted throughout the audience. It
had been organized. All his instincts were to go over
and try to eject the man from the rally, but that
might be exactly what they wanted. If they could

precipitate a brawl, that would undoubtedly mean the end of the meeting.

Susie held up a hand. "Please," she said. "Shortly, I'll introduce Virginia Dare, whom you all love. She has a few words to say to you backing the democratic institutions of Lagrangia."

A voice jeered, "We *used* to love her, back before she sold out to the enemies of the Sons of Liberty!"

Susie flushed. This wasn't going at all well. She was flustered. Never in her life had she been booed before, certainly not in Lagrangia. But now the boos were coming. She was not a public speaker, unused to addressing tens of thousands, many of whom were trying to drown out her voice with their shouts.

All words went out of her head and she stood there, speechless, looking out at them in misery. She had no idea of what to do.

Suddenly, the crowd noise fell to a hush of surprised silence. She didn't understand until, instinctively, she turned.

Bert, Jean and Lonzo were filing up on to the speaker's stand.

Bert approached the microphones and said, his voice dripping with sincerity, "If the other members of the Council have not the courage to address you, Jean, Lonzo and I will do our best."

"Oh, no. No," Susie got out.

But Lonzo said politely, "We will take our turn, Madam Chairwoman. After you have spoken and after Virginia Dare."

She stiffened her back. "No," she said. "I refuse

to share this platform with traitors to all the most sacred institutions of Lagrangia."

"Step down, then," one of the hecklers called. "Let's hear Bert's message!!"

More calls from the crowd said substantially the same thing and then more boos came.

Oh, they're organized all right, King thought, standing at the side of the speaker's stand.

Susie was still hopelessly flustered. How she wished that Rex was here now! No matter that he was no longer a young man. Possibly this was the reason for his being eliminated.

Bert said to her gently, but so that his words went into the mikes, "If you refuse to share the speaker's stand with us, friend Susie, there are the steps over there. Perhaps you and Virginia Dare will prefer to leave."

A hundred voices from the crowd yelled, "Yes. Let's hear the Sons of Liberty!"

Those in the audience who weren't heckling were talking to each other, most at the tops of their voices. It became a Gotterdammerung of sound.

Lonzo, of the Education Function, and the oldest of the three members of the Sons of Liberty, gently took Susie by the arm and led her, as though she were a sleepwalker, to the stairs. King looked up at her emptily as she descended in a daze. He motioned to Virginia Dare who was still sitting on the stand, her eyes wide but determination on her face.

But at his gesture she stood abruptly and marched for the stairs.

When she came up to him, she snapped, "I was going to stay!"

He said wearily, "They would never have let you talk, darling. This has all been set up. By an expert. And I don't have to tell you who I think the expert is."

Chapter Seventeen

Not bothering to summon a hovercar this time, the three of them located bikes and started back for the apartment. King scanned their surroundings, in a hurry to get the two women away. He doubted that they were in danger but with a mob, you never knew. A mob, so he had read, can do things in excitement that no single individual member of it would dream of doing alone. Besides, the crowds were still growing and there were still more uniformed Sons of Liberty, Daughters of Liberty and, yes, the newly formed Youth Auxiliary.

As they rode in depressed silence, Balt came up and joined them on his own bike. He wasn't in Youth Auxiliary uniform. For the nonce he held his peace.

Susie blurted, "But where could the other Council members possibly be?

There was no answer.

Silent, they parked their bikes before the apartment building and ascended the stairs.

Rex, of course, was in his bedroom. He was staring gloomily at the screen of his Tri-Di set. He looked up at their entry and said, "Bert's already finished his talk and Jean's speaking."

At Rex's invitation they took chairs and joined him in what he called his 'turd-watching'.

More and more uniformed Sons of Liberty were arriving, including squads of what King had called storm troopers. They carried batons. Even as the speakers went on, the Sons of Liberty were taking over the rally, in a growing flood.

Rex said, "We were cloddies not to have made some arrangements for policing the park during the meeting. Somehow, we should have rounded up enough supporters of the original Lagrangia system to have made this mess impossible."

"We didn't have time," Susie said bitterly. "The Sons of Liberty have been organizing for at least months. In fact, their nucleus has been in existence for years, since before the declaration of independence from the Reunited Nations."

They watched the balance of the meeting in gloomy silence. In spite of the face that Bert was obviously the leader, and consequently got the most applause, Lonzo was the most effective speaker of the three.

In actuality, none of them said much that hadn't already been revealed in their Tri-Di speeches, their pamphlets and their own organized rallies, all over Lagrangia. When you analyzed it, their program was a negative one. They didn't actually offer firm answers to the problems which confronted the Islands but merely demanded the ending of the

Council as now constituted—and its replacement by the leaders of the Sons of Liberty. Vague promises were made about what the new regime would do. How progress would be resumed, unemployment ended, the birthrate increased, emigration stimulated.

"I wish they'd tell us how," Susie had said bitterly. "If we knew, our present Council would do it."

After the speeches were over, they watched for awhile as the crowd dispersed. There had been a great deal of cheering for Bert, Lonzo and Jean. At its peak, the audience must have numbered nine out of every ten citizens on Grissom.

"It could have been a beautiful rally," Virginia Dare said miserably.

"Well, that does it," King said. "They'll call for the referendum now. Your Council, and all that it stands for, has been repudiated."

But Rex shook his head. "No, not quite yet. They'll want to be doubly sure. They'll spend at least a few days consolidating their victory. Besides, I suspect they're going to want to build up that bullyboy outfit of theirs first. Once they take over, they're going to need a ready and available police force."

There came a knock at the door and Balt went to answer it. He returned accompanied by Werner and Forrest, of the Council.

The others stared at them.

"Where were you?" Susie demanded.

The two looked at her emptily. "Looking into a gunbarrel," Forrest said.

"That's what I suspected," Rex growled. "What happened?"

The two found seats, Forrest appropriating the one Balt had been seated in before the entry of the newcomers. The youth perched at the end of Rex's bed.

"It was cleverly done," Werner said. "Each of us, save Bert, Jean and Lonzo, were phoned and told that a special meeting of the Council was being convened an hour before the rally was scheduled."

"But didn't you suspect anything?" Susie said. "Phoned by whom?"

"By responsible members of each other's staffs. I, for instance, received a call from an assistant on Paul's staff; a fellow I know. It never occurred to me that he might be a member of the Sons of Liberty. Evelyn received a call from one of *my* secretaries, undoubtedly a member of the Daughters of Liberty."

"At any rate, we all attended," Forrest said, in disgust. "And just when we were beginning to smell a rat, eight masked men came in carrying laser pistols."

"Eight?" Rex said. "All with lasers? How do you know that they were laser pistols?"

Forrest said grimly, "The leader cut a corner off that heavy metal conference table."

King said, "Only one fired, eh? The other seven guns were probably mock-ups."

Werner glared at him. "Possibly, but we weren't in any position to find out. At any rate, they held us there until the rally began to break up. We all watched the whole thing on the Tri-Di screen. It was sickening."

Susie said abruptly, "Forrest, you're Councilor of Communications. We'll just put this on the air in every Island of Lagrangia and the sooner the better."

Forrest shook his head wanly. "That was our first reaction but, as the leader of the gunmen pointed out, who'd believe us? It's an unlikely story, at best. Eight men with laser pistols holding practically the whole Council, the governing body of Island Three, at gunpoint for over two hours. Listeners would sneer and claim that the Council had been afraid to stand up and refute the Sons of Liberty. By the way, the leader was the only one who spoke, and he didn't speak Interlingua, he spoke in a slightly accented English."

Rex looked at King.

King said, "Theodor Karadja again."

"Pierre Cannes," Balt murmured.

Rex said to Werner, "Look, am I in good enough shape to get up and go into the living room?"

"Not unless you take it easy. You could stretch out on a couch."

"Wizard," the old detective said. "There's too many of us in this small room and besides I need a drink; I suspect that everybody else does, too. King, give me a hand."

They all filed into the living room and found seats, as Susie went to the bar and called for orders.

When all were served, she turned her eyes to the aged former investigator. "What now?" she said. "We'll never recover from this debacle."

"No," Rex said nastily, "the worm is going to turn."

They all gaped at him.

"What is that supposed to mean?" Forrest said.

"We're going to take the offensive. And the first thing we're going to have to do is ice that goddam Rumanian."

"And his seven men, complete with their lasers," King said sourly. "I can just see us doing it, especially with you laid up."

"I doubt if he's got seven men," Rex told him. "It doesn't make sense for the Soviet Complex to station eight men in Grissom. I doubt if they have eight agents in all Lagrangia. And it's not as though they all came up for this particular assignment; we checked back and found that Pierre Cannes came up alone. Nor have any other tourists from Earthside arrived recently. No, I suspect that five of those eight men were our visitors from Elysium, giving Karadja a helping hand. Two more were probably his agents; Stanley, and whoever the other one might be. My guess is, they didn't want to run *any* risk that you might jump them, so they padded their numbers to scare you. They didn't really want to hurt any of you at this point; but you can bet they won't give a damn when they've recruited plenty of help."

King said, "Even three are bad enough. And, besides, we don't even know where they are. Stanley's been flushed out of his house in Heidi and Karadja has left the Lagrange Hilton. They've gone to ground and, highly trained as they are, we'll never find them."

Rex said, "Damn it, let's have another drink."

While Susie took care of refills, Rex turned to Forrest. "This is where you come in. As head of the Communications Function, aren't you in a position to monitor any tightbeam calls going Earthside?"

"Why, yes."

"All right, then," Rex said. "We know that this Karadja reports to the Soviet Complex. King heard him doing it, in fact, directly to Wladyslaw Kurancheva."

King said, "Yes, but he scrambles the reports."

Rex looked at him. "That's okay," he said. "All we want is to get a fix on wherever he reports from. He's pulled off a major coup today. Tonight, or even sooner, he'll report from wherever he is hiding with his men. Then we'll know where he is."

"Well, that'll be a beginning," Susie said. "He's the key to the whole Sons of Liberty revolt. If we can stop him, we might come up with something that would stymie Bert and his gang."

Forrest went over to the TV phone on the desk and activated it and spent the next ten minutes giving orders. Finally, he turned off the screen and returned to the others.

"All right," he said. "Beginning now, we check out every tightbeam going Earthside, and particularly any that are scrambled to Moscow. As soon as such a message is detected, my people will get an exact fix on the location of the set making it."

"So, all we've got to do is wait," Virginia Dare said.

"Even if we are able to isolate this espionage chap, and I don't see how we can do that, we're still in trouble," Werner said. "If we could come up with some answers to even one or two of the key problems confronting Lagrangia, we might be able to win a referendum on whether or not to make basic changes in our socioeconomic system. Otherwise I'm afraid that we've had it. Why do our Tri-Di broadcasts fall flat on their faces, as compared to those of the Sons of Liberty? Because we have nothing to say. All we can do is repeat over and over again the usual platitudes about democracy."

"And they're not being received very well these days," Susie said. "Who was it that once said, '*Come now, the truth; who among you would be satisfied with justice?*'"

"One of the early science fiction writers," Balt supplied. "Harry Harrison, I believe, in a story called . . ."

"Oh, you and your science fiction," his mother snorted.

Werner checked his wrist chronometer and said, "I'll have to be going. I have a space cafard case at the hospital." He stood.

Forrest got up too and said, "I'd better get on over to the Communications Administration Building and supervise this monitoring."

He turned to Rex. "I'll notify you as soon as anything comes through . . . if it does."

"Wizard," Rex said. "We'll all be here. I still half expect Karadja to take another crack at one or all of us. He's got us on the run but unless I'm badly mistaken, he's not the type to rest on his laurels."

When the two Council members were gone the rest gave up the conversation and went about their business. Susie and Virginia Dare repaired to the kitchen to prepare dinner. Both of them were amateur chiefs, Virginia Dare having picked up her love of gourmet food from the older woman. This household seldom resorted to the food supplied from the automated kitchens of New Frisco. Balt repaired to the extensive bookshelves and the old fashioned hard-cover volumes once accumulated by Professor George Casey.

King sat near Rex, both glum, both wordless.

They finished their drinks and without saying anything King got up and replenished them. Depression evidently counteracted the alcohol; he could feel no effects from the first two, though Susie had mixed them moderately strong.

The call came through shortly before they were ready to sit down to the table.

Susie and Virginia Dare came in and Susie went over to the TV phone on the desk. King, Virginia Dare and Balt stood behind her as she answered.

It was Forrest in the screen, all right, and he looked excited. He said, "Rex was right. The call came through, scrambled and to Moscow. We got a fix on the set being used. Here are the coordinates. Do you have the appropriate map of Grissom?"

"Yes," Susie said, taking up a stylo and edging a paper pad over towards her.

She listed down the letters and numbers he read off to her, flicked off the phone and turned to Rex.

"That was it," she said needlessly. She came to her feet and went over to the bookshelves and brought forth a large folded map and returned with it to the desk. She unfolded it, spread it out and took up her note. She began tracing with a finger, as the others stood around peering down.

"Here it is," she said finally. "About one mile out of New Frisco on Goddard Road, or just off it, at least."

"I know that vicinity," Balt said. "On the edge of the wilderness. Not very many houses; they're spread out all over the place. Small houses, usually only one or two persons occupying them."

They went back to where Rex was stretched out on his couch, looking impatient.

King said, "What now? We know that there are at least three of them and that at least one of them has a laser pistol. Do I go in and shoot it out?" There was a self-deprecation in his voice. "I doubt if it'll be as easy to sneak into this house as it was at Stanley's in Heidi."

"Oh, don't be ridiculous, King," Susie said.

Rex shook his head and said, "No, you can't go in alone. Not up against those pros."

"He won't be alone," Balt said.

Chapter Eighteen

The four older people ogled him.

"What in Zen are you talking about, dear?" Virginia Dare said.

"I'm going too," he said.

Rex took a deep breath and his voice was gentle. "It's a brave gesture, son, but I'm afraid it wouldn't cut the odds down sufficiently. I doubt if you're more experienced in combat than King here, and he admits to never firing a gun in his life until he let off those two rounds by accident."

"I've been hunting ever since I was fourteen years old. I'm a pretty good shot with a rifle."

"We haven't got a rifle."

"Maybe *we* haven't, but *I* have," he said. "A hunting rifle. Also a target pistol."

King said, "I don't feel comfortable about it, Balt."

Balt rapped, "I hope not; look, folks, it's adrenalin time! Even if the present Council retains power, it's not so good if they can't come up with some answers to Lagrangia's problems. If the Sons of Liberty take over, it means we'll be saddled with a dictatorship and we all know what happened in Elysium. And the Sons of Liberty are hand in glove with Elysium. But neither the present Council nor the Sons of Liberty are as much to be feared as the Soviet Complex. And from what King heard in Heidi, the Sons of Liberty are just being used as puppets by this Karadja and his ministry. Just as sure as Zen made little green apples, he has some plan working to take over not only Lagrangia but probably the asteroid belt as well."

Susie said, "You seem to be putting on years, young fellow. Where's the usual sophomoric cynicism?"

He looked her straight in the eye. "Shelved until I need it. Cynicism's for when I can't make a difference or there's not much at stake. But my world is at stake, and I can make more difference than you know."

"It's for all the marbles," Rex admitted. "However, you and King still aren't up to it. If I was on my feet, we might try and come up with something. But I'm not. Two inexperienced men against three well-armed pros equals disaster."

"Oh, I didn't mean just me," Balt said earnestly. "I meant the 150 Club."

"The 150 Club," King blurted. "What in the hell are you talking about?"

Balt's gaze challenged all of them. "A few weeks ago, we formed two subsidiary clubs, The Young People's Hunting Club and The Young People's Karate and Judo Club."

"Holy Jumping Zen," Rex said. "Not to mention you also becoming the Youth Auxiliary of the Sons of Liberty. You youngsters must keep yourselves busy attending meetings."

"That's right," Balt said nodding. "At any rate, all the Hunting Club members have hunting rifles and target pistols."

"How many members in this club?" King demanded.

"Oh, hundreds, altogether."

"Holy Zen," Rex repeated. "An army."

Balt turned his eyes to him. "Oh, we wouldn't all come. That would be redundant and, besides, it'd attract attention. I suggest that fifteen or twenty of our best shots from the older 150 Club members come along."

"But you're just children!" Virginia Dare wailed, aghast.

Rex said to Balt, "How old are these 150 Club members of yours that you'd take along?"

"About seventeen to twenty."

Rex said to Virginia Dare, "Half the men who fought in the American Civil War were that age or younger."

He turned back to the younger man. "Son, you'll have to get on the phone and start rounding up your squad. I'd suggest that you make the attack at first dawn, before the day's activities get underway, and the most likely time that all three of them will be there." He thought about it a moment before adding, "Have you any distinctive uniform or other means of identifying yourselves as Hunting Club members?"

"Yes, we all wear khaki shirts that have 'Young People's Hunting Club' printed on the back."

"Wizard. You can go out in a group, strolling along as though on an outing. You'll be going in the direction of the wilderness, which fits in. Anybody that spots you, and there won't be many people out at that time of day, won't suspect a thing."

Balt and King both nodded at the older man's strategy.

The retired detective said to King, "Go on into the bedroom and get that laser pistol."

When the other had returned with the gun, Rex said, "You'd better take this. I'll check you out on the workings. Given luck, you should be able to scare the pants off them with it. They'll be inside, constricted in their movements. You'll be outside, free to move. But for Zen's sake use all available cover. Remember, a boulder is reclaimed mining slag; it'll stop a handgun laser."

He spent the next fifteen minutes explaining the workings of the pistol, winding up with, "Now, remember, you've only got one power pack. We have no reloads. That means, you've got about one full minute of beam, no more. Usually with a laser pistol, you fire very brief beams to stretch out your power. But you're no marksman. So probably your best bet is to use it like a machete, slashing from left to right, or vice versa. It'd be difficult to miss, unless your target's way off and it shouldn't be. There is no recoil, so you don't have to worry about that."

King, and Balt too, took it all in with care.

Susie said, "We can't put it off forever, let's eat."

Virginia Dare brought Rex a plate and a glass of wine and sat it down next to him on a cocktail table beside the couch, and the others went into the dining room.

In spite of their optimistic plans to eliminate the Soviet contingent, there was still an underlying fear within them all. If they'd come up with this idea a few days earlier, they could have frustrated the enemy before the rally took place, in which case the Sons of Liberty might have been forestalled. But they hadn't.

Susie said lowly, "After this embarrassing reversal, the Council has simply got to come up with some new program that will revive the Lagrangia Islands. As things stand now, the Sons of Liberty seem sure to win their referendum once they demand that it be held."

Balt said, "Couldn't the Council refuse to hold such a referendum?" though he knew the answer before he had asked.

Virginia Dare shook her head. "This is a democracy. Even a comparatively small minority of the Lagrangists can demand a referendum. Once we start making exceptions, we stop having a democracy." She sighed and said, "If only we could get the Island Five Project back underway. It'd keep everybody employed and interested in life for decades."

Susie said, "We all know the answer to that. It'd be a white elephant, a boondoggle. There's nobody to populate it. We haven't been able to populate Island Four. We don't need any more Islands in Lagrangia."

Balt was scowling in memory. "Wait a minute," he said. "Possibly we don't need any more Islands in Lagrangia, but there's something else."

They all turned their eyes to the youngster politely, if not quite patronizingly.

"What, dear?" Virginia Dare said, taking up her wineglass.

"A story I read once."

His mother sighed but didn't interrupt him this time.

He said, "I think it was the first of the type, but I'm not sure. It was called *Universe* and I think it was written by Heinlein. Other stories based on the same general idea were written later, but I think *Universe* was the first."

King said politely, "What was it all about and what has it got to do with Lagrangia's problems?"

"The idea was, this tremendous spaceship was heading for the stars to colonize. It was going to take generations to get there and something happened, a mutiny or something, and the survivors forgot where they were going . . ."

"Now, dear," Virginia Dare said. "I'm sure that the rest of us aren't . . ."

"No, let me go on," her son said urgently. "They also didn't know the nature of the 'world' they were in and had forgotten how to run the starship. The protagonist finally stumbled on the truth and they started up the ship again and got to their destination."

"What's this got to do with Lagrangia's problems?" King said once more.

"Don't you see?" the boy said excitedly. "We

don't build *Island* Five, but we'll build Starship One largely to the same specifications. It won't be a space Island floating without motion in Lagrange Five but will go to the nearest star system where we know the sun is Sol-type and there are planets. Barnard's star is probably it."

They were staring at him now.

He went on excitedly, "It was the original dream! First we were going to seed the solar system with members of the race with I.Q.s of over 130. When the solar system was thoroughly mapped out and largely colonized, advanced technology would allow the human race to reach out into the stars. Well, we got bogged down, so far as the solar system is concerned, but the stars are still beckoning."

"Who'd want to go?" his mother said skeptically.

His words came slowly but definitely. "Lagrangists with I.Q.s of over 150."

They were no longer scornful.

"Why?" Susie said.

"Because it's literally a new world to conquer," he told her. "And those Lagrangists with I.Q.s of over 150 are the most impatient of all about the current slump in activities and ambitions. Nine out of ten with a genius I.Q. want to use it."

Susie said, "Let's go back to the living room and kick this around with Rex."

Rex was as skeptical as any of them had been.

He said, "All right, say that it would solve the unemployment situation—if you could get everybody to agree to participate."

"That'd be no problem," King said. "Your Councils could pass a ruling that anyone who didn't work in the field in which he was experienced would be returned to Earth. Why should Lagrangia put up with parasites? It was you, Rex, that mentioned the old slogan, from each according to his abilities, to each according to his needs. Wizard. Anybody who refuses to use his abilities should be expelled from the society."

Rex said, "All right, it solves one problem, unemployment. But that's only one. And after you'd crewed this overgrown starship, our population would be smaller still."

It was Virginia Dare, looking very thoughtful, who answered that. She said, "No, I think you're wrong. Our immigration has fallen off drastically recently. Why? Because people with I.Q.s of over 130 dislike being stagnant. And those with genius levels of intelligence, even more so. That's why they are currently avoiding Lagrangia. We've become stagnant here, some 95% of the population idle. But given this new dream, there'd be a new influx of ambitious, hard working colonists, including many with I.Q.s exceeding 150 who'd want to go when the star ship was completed."

"I think that Virginia Dare's point is valid," Susie said. "In Professor Casey's day, the adventurous and capable burned to go out to the High Frontier, as some called it. Man has always been intrigued with new frontiers. Well, the stars will become an even newer frontier. And there'll be many an Earthside man and woman who want to share in the new adventure."

"And from the Asteroid Federation as well," Balt said softly.

Rex thought about it. He said, "In actuality, what you're proposing is a gigantic WPA project." He looked at the younger people. "Way before your time. But there was a big depression in America between 1930 and 1940. The government, faced with some fifteen million unemployed, inaugurated make-work projects, to keep the people quiet, largely. I sometimes suspect that the Egyptian pyramids, and possibly the Mexican ones, were much the same thing."

"If we bring this up before the Council, we're going to have to have a pat program to present them with," Balt said, beginning to really get into the thing. "We need a good name for the starship. Island Five is obviously not it, since it won't be an Island. And Starship One is pretty unimaginative."

King laughed and said, "Call it the *Half Moon*."

Rex frowned at him. "Henry Hudson's exploratory ship?"

"No, not exactly, though there's that connotation too. But Island Five, and much of the aerospace engineering necessary has already been done on it, was to be fifteen miles in diameter and seventy-five miles long and have seven thousand square miles of area, about half the size of Switzerland. I submit, to build a starship that size, with materials sent up from Luna, will take half the moon."

They all laughed too.

"Hardly," Susie said. "It's been figured that if all the asteroids were utilized, space colonies 3000 times the area of Earth could be built."

But they accepted the name.

Virginia Dare said, "Do we really need a starship that large?"

"Yes," King said thoughtfully. "We should aim at a million persons to crew it, but they should have ultimate room. They're going to have to take human civilization in all its aspects with them. They're also going to have to take large numbers of every life form useful to man—either on the hoof or in sperm and egg banks. Not just two of each species, such as Noah had in his ark, but a wide enough selection so that a wide variety of genes will be represented."

"That Noah's ark story is one of the silliest in Genesis," Susie said. "He carried two of each type animal and bird. You couldn't have packed them into a ship the size of the old time Queen Mary. And the ark, with its one window, was built by hand by Noah and his sons. They must have worked like demons. But the thing is, there were supposedly two of each type animal. Whoever wrote that story obviously didn't know that there are some 1200 species of lizards alone. Why, it's unlikely that you could have packed every species of the deer family, with their required food, into a vessel the size of the ark."

"I've wondered how the kangaroos, not to speak of the llamas, got to the Near East to join the zoo," Balt said. "Or the South African sloths, who aren't noted for their speed of travel."

"All right, all right, Wizard," Rex said. "Let's get off this Noah's ark kick. Building the *Half Moon* solves several of the problems that have stymied us the last few years. We'll put everybody back to work, not on new Islands and SPSs but on building a starship. There'll be new challenges to our scientists and engineers, there'll be new emigration from Earth. Very well, what's the next step?"

"We'll present it first to the Island Three Council here in Grissom and recommend they request that the Grand Council be convened to study the proposal," Susie said. "As a Council member, I am qualified to call such a meeting."

"That makes sense," Rex nodded. His eyes went to King and Balt. "And now let's get back to how to clobber Comrade Karadja and company. Otherwise, sure as hell, he'll come up with something to foul us up."

Chapter Nineteen

King Ford was giving the chosen members of the Young People's Hunting Club their final briefing in one of the recreation rooms of the 150 Club. There were eighteen of them, besides Balt, all equipped with rifles and holstered target pistols, all wearing the special khaki Hunting Club shirts. They were a bright, earnest group and King was impressed. A little on the young side, as combat men went; the youngest looked to be about sixteen, and the oldest perhaps three years more.

He had a six foot square diagram tacked to the wall.

He pointed to the heavy sheet of paper and said, "This is the layout. Susie, of course, has access to the data banks on the highest priority, as a member of the Council. She got this aerial photo of the vicinity of the house where the three Soviet Complex operatives are hiding. At least, we hope there are only three."

Balt said, "If there were any more than that,

they'd run the chance of being conspicuous to the neighbors. That's a pretty small house."

"There isn't much in the way of neighbors," King said. "But let's hope that you're right."

He went back to the aerial photo. "Now you can see where the target is located, right on the edge of the wilderness, here." He ran a finger over the tress, brush, and grass glens of the area deliberately given over to wildlife, picnicking, hiking, fishing and other nature sports by the Lagrangists.

"As you can see," he went on, "there are only two other houses in the vicinity and even they aren't very close. This area is settled by Lagrangists who like their solitude. However, we checked them out. One is currently not occupied; the other has a couple who by great luck are friends of Werner, Councilor of Medicine. Last night he called them and pretended to have found something in their medical records that disturbed him. He asked them to come immediately to the hospital for some extended tests. That, of course, takes them off the scene, so we'll be free to operate."

He took a deep breath and went on. "We worked this out in detail, last night, with Rex. Here's the plan of action. Behind this little knoll here, in this depression . . ." he touched it with a finger ". . . we'll have our command post. Balt and I will be there. The rest of you will be in three squads of six men each. I suggest that you so divide yourselves now."

The eighteen youths went about dividing themselves into groups of six, evidently having some preferences as to who to go into the fight with.

King said, "And now, each squad elect a squad leader."

That wasn't much more difficult than splitting up into teams. Jim wound up the head of "A" squad, Tom the head of "B" and a tall lanky boy named Gene the corporal of "C". When they reseated themselves, it was by squad.

King said, "Each squad leader will keep in touch with Balt and me and the command post with his pocket transceiver. We have an advantage here. Forrest, of Communications, is one of the Councilors backing us most strongly. He's set up a transmitter across Grissom's diameter that'll blanket this area so that no transceivers and no TV phones are operative other than ours, unless they're keyed for burst-transmission exactly as ours are. In short, the enemy won't be able to summon assistance from either the Elitists or the Sons of Liberty.

"We now get down to the nitty-gritty," he said, taking another deep breath. "Keeping at least twenty feet between you, each squad will zero in on the house. On your bellies, going slowly, using all the cover you see on the map. That suggestion is from Rex, who's been there—been in action, I mean. Don't bunch up. Don't give the enemy a chance to knock several of you over at once."

One of the boys moistened his lips. "Somebody said they have laser pistols. I've read about lasers."

King nodded, unhappily. "That's right. They have at least one, and possibly three, laser pistols. When you're taking cover, crawling nearer, don't make the mistake of hiding behind something like a tree. A laser will cut right through a tree. Be in a

hole, behind a large slag boulder, or behind a hillock with plenty of dirt between you and the house.
When you change positions in your advance, have
your next spot picked out carefully before you make
a dash for it. *Always head for cover.* By the way, I
have a laser too, so all the firepower isn't in their
hands, and they're cooped up."

Jim bobbed his Adam's apple and said, "Look,
we're going out of our way to keep this undercover
but what if somebody comes along? You know,
somebody out for an early morning hike, or something."

King nodded and turned back to the aerial map
and pointed. "There are three roads in the vicinity;
well, paths would be a better word. Each squad will
station one man at one of the paths. His job will be
to intercept anyone looking as though he, or she,
was heading in the direction of the shootout. He'll
explain, politely, that the Young People's Hunting
Club is having a shooting match and that there's
danger of ricochets, so he recommends that they go
no further along that particular path. By that time
we'll be firing aplenty, so the story will sound
authentic."

"When do we start firing?" Tom said.

"When we tell you to from the command post.
Balt or I will fire first, when we've checked you out
and feel you're close enough. Then you come up
with a bang. Every window in the house is to be
broken at the first volley and then continued
rounds are to be fired through them. There are
probably only two doors. Steady fire will also be
directed against them and in such volume that no

man in his right mind would try to come through one of them. The idea is to pin them down."

He looked out the window. "It's getting light. Any questions?"

"Pin them down for how long?" one of the boys said. "As soon as it gets dark, they're going to be able to sneak out. And we're all loaded down with boxes of shells but we can't keep up as heavy a fire as you're talking about all day."

King accepted the validity of the query. "We want them to surrender . . . if we can convince them their position is hopeless. There's one thing to remember about this whole thing. It's a firefight, as they used to call them, assuming what I've read is correct. But, in actuality, those men in the house may not shoot to kill unless we hit one of them first. So let's not be first to hit anybody. The fat would be in the fire for them, if they did. Remember: if possible we want to take them prisoners uninjured so it can be revealed to the Lagrangists that the Sons of Liberty are hand in glove with the Soviet Complex. Then, of course, we'll want to kick them out of Lagrange Five."

"Some war," Balt murmured. "Preferably, no casualties."

"No more questions?" King said. "Wizard, let's go."

The twenty of them filed out of the club rooms and headed for bikes. In a group, they headed for the wilderness, each squad squabbling about who was to be used as the traffic guides on the paths and hence would miss the excitement.

To an outsider, particularly after he had taken in

the inscription on the back of their khaki shirts, the group could be nothing other than a club on an outing. King Ford, the only without rifle or club shirt, hoped he looked sufficiently like an adult supervisor to satisfy a casual glance.

Martha caught up to them just as they were leaving the suburbs and were about to divide into their three squads to approach the target house from different directions. She had a rifle with telescopic sights slung over her shoulder.

"Where in the hell do you think you're going?" Balt snarled.

"With you," she said sweetly.

"Like hell you are," King said, greatly definite.

"Yes, I am," she said. "How'd you stop me? Besides, I'm as good a shot as any of you." She paused and added, "Probably better."

"Aw, come on now, Martha," Tom said. "Damn it, I'm sorry I told you about it."

Balt looked at him in disgust. "Oh, it was you, eh? Blabbing the secrets of the 150 Club."

"She's a club member, too," Tom said defensively.

Balt looked at King. "Two of us can escort her back to the clubhouse and keep her there until it's all over."

"And cut down our firepower?" King groaned. "No, we'll take her along. She can be at the command post with us. We'll be able to keep an eye on her, there."

Meanwhile, inside the solitary house, Theodor Karadja was having a confrontation with his allies of the Sons of Liberty. They had been at it since before dawn and it amounted to a showdown.

The Soviet Complex agents were represented by Frol Pogodin, Vadim Shvets and Karadja himself. The two underlings were stationed at far ends of the room, out of earshot, except for an occasional word spoken in anger.

The Lagrangists were Bert and Jean, and Field Marshal Van Eckmann representing the Elitists.

They had been arguing about the date to call for the referendum. Bert, in particular, was all in favor of putting it off for a week or so until they were sure that they held a majority of the Lagrangist vote. He was one of the opinion that there would never be a second chance. If the space colonists rejected it once, and were given plenty of time to consider all the ramifications, their opportunity would be permanently lost. After all, they'd be voting upon giving away the most extensive liberties a human community had ever enjoyed.

"That's the point," the Rumanian had argued emphatically. "You've got to strike now, while the iron's still hot. Today, the Island Three Council is a laughing stock. But it's still the Council of the most prestigious Island and still backed by such popular figures as Susie Hawkins, Rex Bader and Virginia Dare. Given time, the laughter will die down and there'll be future testimony from them. In actuality, your position isn't tenable."

"Why not?" Jean said. "Of course it is."

"Because you have no more of a program than they have. You've presented no more in the way of answers to Lagrangia's problems than has the

Council. And even a people bored to the point of ennui are going to come to that understanding, sooner or later."

The three revolutionists took that in for a time.

The Soviet agent came to his feet abruptly and went over to the room's center table, picked up a tape cassette and put it into a tape player.

He turned back to them and said, "I keep telling you that you are tyros at this game and we are the most highly experienced revolutionists in history. Sometimes you seem to believe me, but sometimes you don't—let me give you an example."

He turned on the device and shortly a clear voice issued forth. It was that of Jean, reiterating the fact that she didn't trust the Soviet representatives and they'd have to make further plans to go it alone as soon as the Soviet agents had served their purposes. Bert then spoke from the tape, largely backing what she had said, followed by various others of the Central Committee of the Sons of Liberty. The talk couldn't have been more damning.

Karadja flicked off the set in disgust.

"Amateurs," he said. "You didn't even consider being bugged. Why, you have no more aptitude in conspiracy than school children. Do you really think for a moment that you can betray the Soviet Complex? Do not be ridiculous, my friends. You are in this now and will see it through, as agreed."

Bert was smoldering. "See *what* through?" he said. "You haven't even told us what you have in mind. Certainly, you have given us help in our attempt to take over Lagrangia, but you mysteriously hint at some service we're to perform for you once we are in power. Some service that will result in the collapse of the economies of the West. What is it? How can we make decisions about you until we know what it is that you want?"

Karadja returned to his seat and thought about it.

"Very well," he said finally. "Here is the program. After you have assumed power, you will fill your largest space freighter with pulverized bits of a mined asteroid. This automated space-freighter will then secretly be sent out to the geosynchronous orbit which all of the Solar Power Stations are in, the hundreds of them, now beaming their power to Earth. The asteroid debris will be dumped there in an intercept pattern. The freighter will explode—a regrettable accident."

Bert was now scowling at him. "Go on and say the rest of it, if you have the gall."

"The debris will be moving retrograde to the SPSs' orbits. At the speed involved, these comparatively small bits of mass will rip through the fragile stations, destroying every one of them in Earth orbit."

Jean said, "The scheme being to destroy the economies of the West, through depriving them of energy."

"Precisely."

Bert said, his eyes hard: "But what would happen to us then? As you have said, the United States of the Americas has space cruisers. A single one of them could destroy all the Islands in Lagrangia in a day."

The other's grin was vicious. "They will never

suspect you of deliberately destroying a freighter. And who could believe that you would destroy billions of pseudo-dollars worth of your own SPSs?"

The Field Marshal said dourly, "Then they'll know that you're behind it and a nuclear war will break out."

Karadja was still shaking his head. "No, because we too would be deprived of solar power; it would look as though we were slitting our own throats, if we were responsible. Besides, immediately, our Soviet scientists would announce that they had detected a mysterious hail of meteorites approaching the freighter. In fact, they would even produce some of them, claiming they had come from outer space. Their story would be most convincing. No one could suspect other than extraterrestrial origin."

Jean said slowly, "And then the Soviet Complex would go into a crash program to utilize its large fields of petroleum and its array of nuclear fusion plants—an energy reserve that the West can't match. And, very kindly, your government would invite stricken nations to join the Soviet Complex so that their economies could be revitalized."

"Of course," he said, beaming at her.

The Rumanian turned back to Bert. "This, by the way, would solve one of your own immediate problems. Lagrangia would have to go into a crash priority program to build new SPSs. They wouldn't be ready, of course, in time to prevent the economic collapse of the United States and the rest of the West, but it would give your people enough work to last them decades."

Bert said wearily, "It wouldn't work, you know. You couldn't make a credible 'accident' by sending a freighter into exactly that retrograde orbit. It's not my field, but I'm sure you couldn't make everybody buy such an unlikely story."

"It's not my field either," the Rumanian said, impatient with the other. "But this plan originated with Number One himself, and I'm sure that his science advisors are not fools. Besides, it is a fact that Halley's comet orbits around the sun in retrograde, so why couldn't a rogue cluster of meteorites do the same?"

Bert said sourly, "As far as Number One's science advisors are concerned, wasn't it Stalin who had Lysenko as one of his top proteges?"

Frol Pogodin, stationed to one side of the window at the room's far end, called suddenly, "There's someone out there, Comrade Major."

"Doing what?" the Rumanian snapped.

"Crawling up toward the house. And, yes! There's more than one of them!"

Chapter Twenty

Theodor Karadja was on his feet instantly, darting to the window beside which his underling was stationed. His hand flashed into his jacket and was suddenly equipped with a laser pistol.

He took his place on the other side of the window. "Where?" he rasped.

Pogodin said, "There's at least three of them, perhaps more. They take turns at advancing. See that large boulder, about seventy meters out? There's one of them behind that."

"Do you have any idea at all who they might be? You're a Lagrangist."

"They're carrying rifles and seem to be wearing an informal uniform. But I know of no . . ."

One of the boys took that moment to pop out of a gully and dashed, bent low, forward to the shelter of a small hillock.

"That makes four," Pogodin growled.

Karadja called across the room to Vadim Shvets, "Do you see anything?"

"Yes," the other agent called back. He too had a laser pistol in his hand. "A man just broke from an outcropping of rocks, dashed forward about six meters and disappeared into a fold in the ground."

"What in the name of Zen's going on?" Bert blurted, coming to his feet and starting in the direction of the window where the Rumanian was stationed.

"Stay where you are!" Karadja snapped at him.

Keeping out of the line of fire offered by the window, he returned to the two Island Three Councilors and the Elitist.

He said, his voice urgent, "The house is surrounded by armed men. Who could they be?"

"Armed men?" Jean said. "Don't be ridiculous. There are no armed men in Grissom save yourselves. And I still don't know where you got those laser pistols you carry."

"We made them," the espionage ace grated. "And just for your information, the other night Stanley's house in Heidi was prowled by someone I suspect was King Ford. When I detected him, he fired at me twice. I dug a Gyro-jet slug out of the wall, so Grissom isn't as free of firearms as all that. Who could those men out there be?"

They looked at him without response. Jean shook her head negatively.

Shvets said, "So far, I've seen three of them. They're working closer. Should I fire on them, Comrade Major?"

"No," Karadja said in irritation. "Not yet."

Bert said, "But this is impossible. There are no groups of a military or police nature in Lagrangia."

"Could they have come up from Earthside, a group of the American military, or their IABI?"

"Certainly not," Bert said indignantly. "I'm Councilor of Transportation. I'd be the first to know."

The agent ran the back of his left hand over his mouth in fustration. This didn't add up at all. He went over to the window where Shvets was stationed and stood to one side, carefully, while looking out.

"They're getting closer," Shvets said nervously. "I can see the back of one of them. The hole he's in isn't deep enough. They haven't had the training we get in the KGB. Should I nail him, Comrade Major?"

"Shut up," Karadja rasped. "I've got to think. We're not under fire yet."

He turned and said to Bert, "Get on your transceiver. Call your Sons of Liberty Guards. If any of them have sporting rifles, tell them to bring them. We're a mile out of town. They'll get here in time . . ."

Bert had his pocket transceiver in hand and spoke into it. Its tiny speaker responded only with a hiss of white noise. He stared down blankly and said, "It's not working. But it always works."

Jean was already on her way to the TV phone on the desk. She flicked its switch, tried the receiver mode. White noise greeted her. Then she turned back to the others, as surprised as Bert.

"The phone isn't working either," she told them. "But I've never heard of such a thing. We've been isolated. But it's impossible. Whoever's responsible, I object to this cavalier . . ."

The Rumanian rasped, "Who could have done that? Blanketed this house?"

Bert said, still unbelievingly, "Why, it'd have to go to the highest echelons of the Communications Function. In fact, it would have to be ordered by Forrest himself. No one else could take the responsibility for such a thing."

"And Forrest is in Rex Bader's camp, eh? That means those men out there are working under the orders of Bader, Susie and the others."

He ran his left hand over his mouth again, thinking desperately.

Finally, he said, "All right. You three leave. Go on out, get your bicycles and return to New Frisco."

"Are you drivel-happy?" Jean said. "You said the house is surrounded and that the men involved have rifles."

"They won't shoot *you*. I doubt if they even know that you're here. You two are Council members." He turned his eyes to the Field Marshal. "And you're an honored guest from Elysium. They won't harm you, either. If they harmed any of you in any manner, it would be the end of them. A referendum would immediately end the government of the Council and your people would be in. So go on and leave. As you go, pretend not to see any of them. Get into New Frisco immediately and send out as many of your Sons of Liberty guards as you can locate. This time Rex Bader and King Ford have gone too far. When the news breaks of what they've done here, it'll be the end of them."

Bert shot a look at the others. "I think he's right," he said. "They wouldn't dare harm us. I suspect that Rex discovered where Pierre Cannes was in hiding and sent these men to get him. He's right, they probably don't even know that we're here."

Outside, behind the knoll where King and Balt had their command post, King was staring at the house through a pair of binoculars Rex Bader had supplied him with. Balt had his head down and Martha sat at the bottom of the hole, her gun across her knees, a satisfied smirk on her face.

"When do we start shooting?" she said.

"Quiet, you cloddy," Balt growled at her. "What's up, King?"

"There are six bikes in front of the house," the other told him, less than happily. "Which undoubtedly means six persons inside. If they're all armed with lasers, they'll cut us to ribbons."

Balt put his head up cautiously to take a look.

"Just a minute," King said, "the front door is opening."

Balt said, "Three of them. Holy Zen, one's a woman. Why, I know her. That's Jean! She's Councilor of the Statistics Function."

"And one of the others is Bert. I can recognize that sandy hair. But who's the third one?"

"That's Field Marshal Van Eckmann," Balt said, as the three left the house and approached the bike rack. "He's one of the bastards from Elysium. Their leader, in fact."

Martha was beside them now, her own head cautiously over the top of the depression.

"You going to let them get away?" she said to King.

He looked at her in disgust. "What can we do? It's one thing coming out here to apprehend three Soviet Complex agents, meddling in the internal affairs of Lagrangia. But two of those people are members of Island Three's governing body, and the third is a member of the government of Elysium."

They watched as the three mounted their bikes and started down the path in the direction of New Frisco.

King groaned. "If they have any idea we're here, they'll send back an army of Sons of Liberty."

"Then we'd better get moving," Martha said reasonably. She threw the bolt of her light hunting rifle.

King ignored her and took up his pocket transceiver and dialed Rex. He said into the tiny screen, his voice crisp, "Bert, Jean, and Van Eckmann just left the house. They could be heading back for New Frisco after a conference."

Rex's voice, tiny but clear, came back. "Did you get a photo of them?"

"Photo?" King said. "I haven't even got a camera."

"But I have," Martha said sweetly. "A mini-mini, and I got three shots of them just as they were leaving."

King sighed and said into the transceiver, "Yeah, we got three shots of them."

"Are the boys near enough to be in range with those light caliber guns of theirs?"

"They should be."

"Then you'd better start the fireworks," Rex said, his face fading.

King took a deep breath and, in turn, called his three squad leaders, giving them the same message. He said, "See that you're all in the safest cover you can find. Once the firing begins, stay put. Don't try to get any closer. We don't want any heroes. Don't expose yourselves to their lasers."

He flicked off the instrument and turned to Balt. "Let's start the ball rolling. Put a bullet through that largest window."

Balt brought his rifle up, threw a cartridge into the firing chamber, steadied his aim and squeezed the trigger. The window didn't shatter at the first shot but as the fusillade from the rest of the boys began striking the building, one by one the windows collapsed.

Balt threw another bullet into the breech and grinned at King. "You know," he said, "those cloddies in there aren't going to know that these bullets we're using are only twenty-twos."

Martha had made herself comfortable, her rifle over the top of the depression. She squeezed the trigger gently.

King said to her, "What are you aiming at?"

"The tires on those bicycles," she said calmly. "Just in case they make a break for it."

"At this distance?" He put his binoculars back to his eyes. "Holy Zen," he said. "You've already flattened two of them."

"I told you I was the best shot in the outfit."

Balt said, steadily firing, "They don't seem to be replying. How would we know, if they did?"

"Search me," King told him. "I've never fired a laser, or seen one fired. I think possibly Karadja took a shot at me in Heidi, but I'm not sure. I was scared silly."

The rattling of the hunting rifles continued. All windows had been broken, the doors peppered unmercifully.

King looked down the road toward New Frisco. It was only a little over a mile into town and it'd take precious little time for Bert, Jean and Van Eckmann to get there.

"We've got to do something," he said. "We haven't got as much time as we thought we were going to have."

He looked at the house thoughtfully. It was two-storied and had a peaked roof of what looked like shale, at this distance. Inspiration came.

"I'll be damned," he said.

He brought out the laser pistol Rex had given him and, very carefully, rested it on a small boulder before him. He flicked off the safety and, following the retired detective's instructions as well as he could remember them, aimed, pressed the trigger and swept the gun from left to right.

The roof of the bungalow, sheared through, collapsed into the room of the second floor.

"Wow," Balt said. "That'll give them something to think about."

King wet his lips. "I hope nobody was on the second floor," he said. "The idea was to avoid casualties."

"Why in the name of Zen aren't they firing back?" Martha muttered, coolly reloading.

"Yeah," Balt said.

King said, "I suspect that they're trying to avoid casualties as well. That Karadja, in there, is a sharp number. And he's got even more to lose than we have. At least, you people are Lagrangists."

It was then that a white pillow case, tied onto a stick, was thrust out the front door and waved.

"They're surrendering!" Balt said excitedly.

The firing fell off completely.

The door opened and three men filed out, their hands high over their heads.

King said, "Let's go," and came to his feet.

They started toward the house. King kept his laser pistol in hand, Balt and Martha with their rifles at the ready.

But there was no treachery. The three Soviet Complex agents stood there, hands still high.

By the time King, Balt and Martha were within a few yards, more of the youths were coming up, led by Jim, Tom and Gene. They too had their weapons at the ready.

The Rumanian stared in astonishment at the age of the others but got out an indignant, "What is the meaning of this?"

King said, "Search them."

Three of the 150 Club boys advanced and carefully frisked the three prisoners. They came up with practically nothing.

King scowled and said, "Where are your guns?"

"What guns?" Karadja said indignantly. "I don't know what you have in mind but these two gentlemen are citizens of Lagrangia and I'm a tourist from Common Europe, visiting Philip, here in his home. My name is Pierre Cannes and I demand . . ."

"Your name is Theodor Karadja and you're not from Common Europe, you're an agent from the Soviet Complex attempting to overthrow the legal government of Lagrangia," Balt said flatly. "*Now* what do you demand, spook?"

"Prove it."

King said to Balt, "Take ten of your men and search the house. Proof that they had lasers is enough to expel them from Lagrange Five. Undoubtedly, they've hidden them."

Balt led the ten into the house.

King got out his transceiver and called Rex again. When the older man's face had faded in, he said, "Mission accomplished. We've got all three of them under gunpoint. However, they're unarmed. They didn't fire back when we attacked and now they deny having any arms."

Rex scowled and thought about it.

The Rumanian laughed nastily. He shrugged and said, "It's no crime to travel under a pseudonym. I admit my real name isn't Pierre Cannes, but that is no business of yours. Meanwhile, you have attacked us, at great danger to our lives and damage to the home of my friend Philip."

Balt and his crew came out of the house, their faces empty.

Balt said, "We couldn't find any lasers, or any other kind of gun for that matter."

"Of course not," Karadja said.

King looked plaintively at Rex in the tiny screen of the pocket transceiver. "No guns," he said.

"Balls," Rex told him. "I'm getting in touch with Forrest. He'll be out with metal detectors that could locate a metallic paperclip. Those guns are hidden somewhere in that house, probably in a secret cache."

Karadja took his chance. He probably realized that this gang of kids had never shot anybody in their collective lives and all of their instincts would prevail upon them not to do it now, no matter what the circumstances. He dashed, taking evasive action, zig-zagging down the road toward New Frisco, desperately hoping to run into a rescuing force of Sons of Liberty, or at least a bicycle left somewbere by the 150 Club boys before their attack.

The boys and King stared after him, in surprised shock.

It was Martha who calmly sat down on the ground, put her elbows on her knees, took careful aim and sent him sprawling.

"Holy Jumping Zen!" King blurted in protest. "You've killed him!"

"Naa," Martha said in satisfaction. "You don't kill anybody by shooting him in the calf of the leg with a twenty-two."

She stood again as half a dozen of the boys hurried to recapture the fallen espionage ace, who was sitting on the ground now, grimacing in disgust and fondling his leg.

Balt looked at Martha, twisted his face in deprecation and said, "Knock, knock."

"Oh, no you don't," she said. "Knock, knock yourself."

He frowned, but answered, "Who's there?"

"Amsterdam."

"Amsterdam who?"

"Amsterdam sick and tired of your knock-knock jokes."

Chapter Twenty-One

The hover car pulled up before the Island Three Administration Building. King, Balt, and Virginia Dare emerged from the front seat and Susie from the rear. The two men came around and helped a shaky Rex to the sidewalk, where Susie supported him, while King and Balt wrestled a folded wheelchair from the back of the car and deployed it.

The retired detective seated himself. King pushed Rex through the lobby to the flights of stairs leading up to the sixth floor and their destination, while Virginia Dare gave a helping hand from behind. Susie followed along worriedly.

Rex growled, "You're lucky I don't weigh any more than an old man should."

"You weigh enough," King told him.

They rested at each floor and finally made it to the sixth where King took over again.

At the Council's Conference Room, Balt opened the door, perhaps a bit dramatically, and the wheelchair went through.

The Council, all twenty of them including Bert, Jean and Lonzo, were in the process of seating themselves. All looked up, most of them in surprise.

Bert snapped, "What is the meaning of this intrusion? This is a formal meeting of the Council of Island Three. Outsiders are not permitted except by invitation. Is that clear?"

"Werner and I invited them," Forrest said dryly. "They are to testify on something of interest to the Council."

Bert looked grumpy but said nothing further. Virginia Dare, King and Balt took seats together. Rex, in his wheelchair, was directly behind them. Susie, as a Council member, took her usual place.

Jean said, "I nominate Bert as the afternoon's chairman."

"Second the motion," Lonzo said.

Susie laughed softly at the attempt and said, "I nominate Forrest."

"Second," Paul said.

Only Jean and Lonzo voted for their leader. Forrest took over the chairman's seat and tapped the gavel lightly.

He looked around at them and said, "It is understood that a plan has surfaced to revitalize Lagrangia, end unemployment, and spark new advances in science and technology."

"What plan?" Bert said in irritation. "I demand that the meeting begin with a proprosal Jean, Lonzo and I have drawn up for a referendum to be voted upon by all Lagrangians."

"That is your right," Forrest nodded. "But unless there is a protest on the part of the majority, the *first* order of business shall be the new plan for revitalization."

The majority did not protest.

The Communications Councilor said, "Very well. Since our Honorary Councilor, Susie, is privy to the new plan, she'll address us upon it and later answer our questions."

Susie spend the next half hour explaining the *Half Moon* project, the germ of which had originally been hit upon by young Balt.

When she finally came to a halt, all eyes were on her.

Bert blurted, "Are you mad? You'd drain the best brains of Lagrangia and Earth to crew this white elephant and blast them out into deep space?"

"And the Asteroid Federation as well," King said mildly. "I am sure that many of us of the asteroid Islands who have the necessary qualifications will be keen to go as well."

Bert said, "Isn't it bad enough that we have less than three million population, our birth rate is falling off, and emigration has slowed to a trickle? You'd rob us of one third of our population, our best brains at that, in this scatterbrained scheme?"

Susie said, "How quaint to hear *you* use the word, 'scheme', Councilor. But it's a new dream for the human race; nothing less than colonization of the stars. Not only will Lagrangia be revitalized, but Earth as well—and hundreds of thousands will clamor to be allowed to become space colonists. You've heard the old cliche about steam engines coming when it's steam engine time?" Her eyes were shining. "Well, when we announce the plan I think we'll find, at last, that it's starship time . . ."

Werner, who had been in on some of the sessions devoted to smoothing out the details of the *Half Moon* project, said, "And the project could also be utilized to raise the birthrate. We could publicize the great glory that will come to the parents of the star pioneers—and since it'll take a generation to build the *Half Moon*, most of those pioneers *haven't been born*! Get it? This will be an incentive for Lagrangists to bear and raise children. And not all of 'em will be crewing the *Half Moon*."

Bert was flabbergasted and, for the time, held his peace.

Evelyn said thoughtfully, "The idea has its possibilities and I'm inclined to think it should be brought before the Grand Council of Lagrangia for debate. However, there's one bothersome aspect. It has been estimated that even with the most modern automation and computerization it would take twenty-five years to build Island Five. Since the plans for the Half Moon are based on the preliminary work done in Island Five, I assume it would take the same length of time. Now the question becomes: what happens when the project has been successfully concluded? Do we enter into stagnation again?"

Jerry, of Research, looked over at her. "The obvious answer is that we immediately begin construction of *Half Moon Two*."

"And milk the solar system of another million geniuses!" Bert said indignantly.

Jerry said, as to a fool, "Exactly. By that time, a

new generation of motivated, intelligent men and women will have reached maturity. If man is going to colonize the stars, and I believe that is his ultimate destiny, a *dozen* ships are not enough. We'll have to continue to build more. Perhaps something will happen to the original *Half Moon*—we don't know—but if we are to colonize the galaxy, it will be because we send starship after starship, down through the centuries."

Jean said, aghast, "Sending our best brains out and leaving the dregs behind! Those of us remaining would develop a racial inferiority complex."

Susie shook her head. "That was the original idea in seeding Lagrange Five and the asteriod belt. We demanded a minimum I.Q. of 130 and left the rest behind, Earthside. We even developed a contemptuous name for them, earthworms. Now the shoe will be on the other foot. Even most of us here will be part of what you call the dregs left behind when mankind erupts into the stars."

Li, the little Chinese, said, "But what do you expect to find out there?"

King said, "Challenges. Obviously, we don't know what form they'll take. Perhaps even other intelligent life forms."

Lonzo spoke up for the first time. "Nonsense. If there were other intelligent life forms out there, why haven't they gotten in touch with us?"

It was young Balt who said, "Perhaps, thus far at least, they haven't given a damn because they're so far beyond us. In a story by Mark Twain, *The Mysterious Stranger*, the stranger describes how the more advanced life forms feel about humanity. As an example, he used a line of ants walking along a railroad track. The engineer of the locomotive coming along has nothing against them but he most certainly isn't going to stop the train, if he finds out they're there. He just doesn't give a damn."

Werner laughed shortly and said, "There are other possibilities. Perhaps, becoming compassionate after a few million years of advanced civilization, they *do* give a damn. They don't contact us because they don't want to, ah, louse up our fledgling civilization as we did to the Tasmanians. They became so frustrated at how much more the white man was advanced over their institutions that they deliberately stopped breeding."

Forrest said, "This sort of speculation could go on for hours. I suspect that the consensus here is that we place the *Half Moon* project before the Grand Council of all the Islands and meanwhile that we study up on the subject, both individually and in conjunction."

Somebody made a motion to the effect and it passed, only the three Sons of Liberty demurring.

Bert was staring at young Balt, and not with good will. "What in the hell are you doing here?" he said. "You're the head of the Youth Auxiliary of the Sons of Liberty."

Balt's eyes were cool and level. "I used to be," he said. "The Youth Auxiliary is disbanding. We're going to issue one final statement to the effect that we're pulling out because the Sons of Liberty have nothing to do with liberty and hence isn't a movement that we can support."

Bert glared at the youth but wasted no further

words on him. Instead he spun on Forrest and said, "I request that we now discuss the referendum."

Before the chairman could answer, Rex said, "Before you do, I have some information to impart."

"You're not a member of this Council!" Bert said, his voice cold.

"But he has been invited to testify," Susie said.

Forrest tapped his gavel. "Very well, Rex. What have you got to say before we discuss the matter of the referendum on the Sons of Liberty?"

Rex, his eyes on Bert, spoke with the wry, measured pace of a man enjoying himself. "Your three Soviet Complex colleagues have defected. Obviously, having failed, they didn't dare return to Moscow. They have been granted asylum here in return for testifying on their activities in support of the Sons of Liberty and against the basic institutions of Lagrangia. Even Theodor Karadja, Wladyslaw Kurancheva's fair-haired boy, would rather not go home. He'd rather talk about you and your mutual conspiracy, Bert."

"I deny it all. I've never heard of them."

King said mildly, "I'm glad to hear you say so. No doubt you can explain away our witnesses and photographs of you leaving their house. Do you have door-to-door salesmen on Grissom, Councilor?"

Rex smiled at King's sarcasm, adding, "There's still more damning evidence. Five emissaries from the Elitist dictatorship in Elysium have been here conferring with you. Some time ago they received shipments of arms, forwarded from Earthside to

Lagrangia and then transshipped. With them they overthrew the legal government of Elysium and, with them, remain in power. I doubt if there is anyone else in Lagrangia who could have arranged the transshipment. You're the Councilor of Transportation and hence in charge of the freighters that run out to the asteroid belt. I have no doubt that you've tried to cover your tracks, but somewhere along the line there must be material in the data banks that will show you up."

Bert was glaring at him.

Rex said gently, "I doubt if I'll ever find proof for this last item but some time ago a few shots were taken at me out in the wilderness. King was a witness but we didn't see the would-be assassin. He was an amateur, or he would have finished me. I suggest that, early in the game, you decided that I was one of your prime obstacles and decided to get me out of the way. I suggest that either you, or one of your Sons of Liberty bully boys, took those shots at me."

"It's a lie," Bert said.

"Of course," said Susie with smooth mockery. "However, when it's all turned over to the Tri-Di news commentators, it all amounts to quite a bit of adverse publicity, Bert. If you don't mind a bit of friendly advice: maybe you should find someone else to ramrod your referendum; I mean someone who will have a *little* credibility twenty-four hours from now."

Aftermath

They were stretched out on their backs, side by side, their hands tucked behind their heads and both staring at the ceiling. Virginia Dare said, "So, tomorrow you're leaving?"

"That's right," King told her.

"The job is accomplished."

"I suppose so. Bert has been exposed as the Lagrangist responsible for transshipping the arms. The Sons of Liberty have been exposed as planning a major coup in conjunction with the Elitists. Both have been discredited."

"But your danger in the Asteroid Federation still remains. The Elitists are ruthless—and armed."

He smiled softly, as though at inner thoughts. "Not exactly," he said. "Those former anarchists weren't as inefficient as we gave them credit for. I just got a tightbeam from my father a few hours ago. The Elitists have been overthrown."

She came to one elbow and stared down at him.

"Overthrown! But they had weapons and the people didn't."

"Solidarity is a weapon, too. Evidently those former anarchists had some old traditions to call upon. In short, sabotage and the general strike. The Elitists never knew what hit them. The American president, Madison, once said that a nation doesn't stand upon bayonets. The Elitists controlled the armories, the police and the army, but they didn't control the sources of food, clothing, shelter, transportation, communications, distribution, medicine and all the rest of the absolute necessities that any society must have to operate. When the people got fed up enough, they simply sat down—except for some of the more excitable ones who resorted to sabotage. The Elitists crumbled."

"Wonderful, but what kind of a system prevails now? They haven't gone back to anarchy, have they?"

"No. Evidently, there's still quite a bit of confusion but I assume that, with the aid of the other Islands in the Federation, the dust will settle shortly."

After a silence, Virginia Dare said softly, "I'm surprised, King, that you haven't asked me to go along with you."

He looked over at her. "I would have, darling. But you see, I have the qualifications to become a senior crew member of the *Half Moon* when it's completed in twenty-five years. I understand that you, ah, wouldn't choose to try and qualify. I intend to go, Virginia Dare."

"I see. I assume that Balt will go too."

He chuckled. "Go? Hell, that monster will probably be captain. Without doubt that whole 150 Club of his will volunteer en masse."

She said softly still, "If you intend to skim off so many of our best and brightest, the least you could do is sire some of them yourself, King."

He grunted in surprise. "Hadn't considered that. For all I know, my kids wouldn't want to go."

"Some might not. They'd have a whole generation to make that decision—and I've made *my* decisions already, if you're willing."

He looked over at her again and cocked his head questioningly. "What does that lead up to?"

"I'll settle for the twenty-five years, my love."